The Iron Tactician

The Iron Tactician

Alastair Reynolds

NewCon Press
England

First published in the UK by NewCon Press
41 Wheatsheaf Road, Alconbury Weston, Cambs, PE28 4LF
December 2016

NCP 109 (limited edition hardback)
NCP 110 (softback)

10 9 8 7 6 5 4 3 2 1

ISBN:

978-1-910935-29-3 (hardback)
978-1-910935-30-9 (softback)

Cover art by Chris Moore
Cover layout by Andy Bigwood

Minor Editorial meddling by Ian Whates
Book layout by Storm Constantine

Merlin felt the old tension returning. As he approached the wreck his mouth turned dry, his stomach coiled with apprehension and he dug nails into his palms until they hurt.

He sweated and his heart raced.

'If this was a trap,' he said, 'it would definitely have sprung by now. Wouldn't it?'

'What would you like me to say?' his ship asked, reasonably.

'You could try setting my mind at ease. That would be a start. It's one of ours, isn't it? You can agree with me on that?'

'It's a swallowship, yes. Seven or eight kiloyears old, at a minimum estimate. The trouble is, I can't get a clean read of the hull registry from this angle. We could send out the proctors, or I could just sweep around to the other side and take a better look. I know which would be quicker.'

'Sometimes I think I should just let you make all the decisions.'

'I already make quite a lot of them, Merlin – you just haven't noticed.'

'Do whatever you need to do,' he said, bad-temperedly.

As *Tyrant* swooped around the wreck, searchlights brushed across the hull like delicate, questing fingertips, illuminating areas of the ship that would have been in shadow or bathed only in the weak red light of this system's dwarf star. The huge wreck was an elaborate flared cylinder, bristling with navigation systems and armaments. The cylinder's wide mouth was where it sucked in interstellar gas, compressing and processing it for fuel, before blasting it out the back in a vicious, high-energy exhaust stream. Swallowships were ungainly, and they took forever to get up to the speed where that scoop mechanism was effective, but there was nowhere in the galaxy they couldn't reach, given time. Robust, reliable and relatively easy to manufacture, there had been only minor changes in design and armaments across many kiloyears. Each of these ships would have been home to thousands of people, many of whom would live and die without ever setting foot on a world.

There was damage, too. Holes and craters in the hull. Half the cladding missing along one great flank. Buckling to the intake petals, beyond anything a local crew could repair.

Something had found this ship and murdered it.

'There,' *Tyrant* said. 'Swallowship *Shrike*, commissioned at the High Monarch halo factory, twelve twelve four, Cohort base time, assigned to deterrent patrol out of motherbase Ascending Raptor, most recently under command of Pardalote... there's more, if you want it.'

'No, that'll do. I've never been near any of those places, and I haven't heard of Pardalote or this ship. It's a long way from home, isn't it?'

'And not going anywhere soon.'

Beyond doubt the attacking force had been Husker. Whereas a human foe might have finished this ship off completely, the Huskers were mathematically sparing in their use of force. They did precisely enough to achieve an end, and then left. They must have known that there were survivors still on the ship, but the Huskers seldom took prisoners and the continued fate of those survivors would not have concerned them.

Merlin could guess, though. There would have been no chance of rescue this far from the rest of the Cohort. And the damaged ship could only have kept survivors alive for a limited time. A choice of deaths, in other words: some slow, some fast, some easier than others.

He wondered which he might have chosen.

'Dig me out a blueprint for that mark of swallowship, the best you can, and find a docking port that places me as close as possible to the command deck.' He touched a hand to his sternum, as if reminding himself of his own vulnerability. 'Force and Widsom, but I hate ghost ships.'

'Then why are you going in?'

'Because the one thing I hate more than ghost ships is not knowing where I am.'

The suit felt tight in places it had never done before. His breath fogged the faceplate, his lungs already working double-time. It had been weeks since he had worn the suit, maybe months, and it was telling him that he was out of shape, needing the pull of a planet's gravity to give his muscles something to work against.

'All right,' he said. 'Open the lock. If I'm not back in an hour, find a big moon and scratch my name on it.'

'Are you sure you don't want the proctors to accompany you?'

'Thanks, but I'll get this done quicker on my own.'

He went inside, his suit lit up with neon patches, a moving blob of light that made his surroundings both familiar and estranged at the same time. The swallowship was huge but he only meant to travel a short distance through its innards. Up a level, down a level, each turn or bend taking him further from the lock and the debatable sanctuary of his own ship. He had been steeling himself for corpses, but so far there were none. That meant that there had been survivors. Not many, perhaps, but enough to gather up the dead and do something with their bodies.

Slowly Merlin accepted that the ship was all that it seemed, rather than a trap. The suit was beginning to seem less of a burden, and his breathing had settled down. He was nearly at the command deck now, and once there it would not take him long to decide if the ship held useful information.

He needed better charts. Recently there had been a few close scrapes. A couple of turbulent stretches had damaged *Tyrant*'s syrinx, and now each transition in and out of the Waynet had Merlin praying for his last shred of good luck. Swallowships could not use the Waynet, but any decent captain would still value accurate maps of the old network. Its twinkling corridors of accelerated spacetime provided cover, masking the signature of a ship if it moved on a close parallel course. The location of the Waynet's major hubs and junctions was also a clue as to the presence of age-old relics and technological treasure.

Merlin paused. He was passing the doorway to one of the frostwatch vaults, where the surviving crew might have retreated as the last of their life-support systems gave out. After a moment's hesitation he pushed through into the vault. In vacuum, it was no colder or more silent than any other space he had passed through. But he seemed to feel an additional chill as he entered the chamber.

The cabinets were stacked six high on opposite walls of the vault, and the vault went on much further than his lights could penetrate. Easily a hundred or more sleepers in just this vault, he decided, but there would be others, spread around the ship for redundancy. Thousands in total, if the swallowship was anything like his own. The status panels next to each cabinet were dead, and when Merlin swept the room with a thermal overlay, everything was at the same low temperature. He drifted along the cabinets, tracing the names engraved into the status panels with his fingertips. Sora… Pauraque… they were common Cohort names, in some cases identical to people he had known. Some had been colleagues or friends; others had been much more than that. He knew that if he searched these vaults long enough he was bound to find a Merlin.

It had not been such a rare name.

One kindness: when these people went into frostwatch, they must have been clinging to some thought of rescue. It would have been a slim hope, but better than none at all. He wanted to think that their last thoughts had been gentle ones.

'I'm sorry no one came sooner,' Merlin whispered, although he could have shouted the words for all the difference they made. 'I'm too late for you. But I'm here to witness what happened to you, and I promise you'll have your justice.'

Filled with disquiet, he left the vault and made his way to the command deck. The control consoles were as dead and dark as he had been expecting, but at least there were no bodies. Merlin studied the consoles for a few minutes, satisfying himself that there were no obvious booby-traps, and then spooled out a cable from his suit sleeve. The cable's end was a standard Cohort fixture and it interfaced with the nearest console without difficulty.

At first all was still dead, but the suit was sending power and data pulses into the console, and after a few minutes the console's upper surface began to glow with faint-but-brightening readouts. Merlin settled into a chair with his elbow on the console and his fist jammed under his helmet ring. He expected a long wait before anything useful could be mined from the frozen architecture. Branching diagrams played across his faceplate, showing active memory registers and their supposed contents. Merlin skimmed, determined not to be distracted by anything but the charts he had come for. The lives of the crew, the cultural records they carried with them, the systems and worlds this ship had known, the battles it had fought, might have been of interest to him under other circumstances. Now was the time for a ruthless focus.

He found the navigation files. There were thousands of branches to the tree, millions of documents in those branches, but his long familiarity with Cohort data architecture enabled him to dismiss most of what he saw. He carried on searching, humming an old Plenitude tune to cheer himself up. Gradually he slowed and fell silent. Just as disappointment was beginning to creep in, he hit a tranche of Waynet maps that were an improvement on anything he had for this sector. Within a few seconds the data was flowing into his suit and onward to the memory cores of his own ship. Satisfied at last, he made to unspool.

Something nagged at him.

Merlin backtracked. He shuffled up and down trees until he found the set of records that had registered on his subconscious even as his thoughts had been on the charts.

Syrinx study and analysis

Beneath that, many branches and sub-branches relating to the examination and testing of a fully active syrinx. A pure cold shiver ran through him.

Something jabbed into his back, just below the smooth hump of his life-support unit. Merlin did the only thing that he could, under the circumstances, which was to turn slowly around, raising his hands in the age-old gesture. The spool stretched from his glove, uncoupled, whisked back into its housing in the wrist.

Another suit looked back at him. There was a female face behind the visor, and the thing that had jabbed him was a gun.

'Do you understand me?'

The voice coming through in his helmet spoke Main. The accent was unfamiliar, but he had no trouble with the meaning. Merlin swallowed and cleared his throat.

'Yes.'

'Good. The only reason you're not dead is that you're wearing a Cohort suit, not a Husker one. Otherwise I'd have skipped this part and blown a hole right through you. Move away from the console.'

'I'm happy to.'

'Slowly.'

'As slow as you like.' Merlin's mouth felt dry again, his windpipe tight. 'I'm a friend. I'm not here to steal anything, just to borrow some of your charts.'

'Borrowing, is that what you call it?'

'I'd have asked if there was anyone to ask.' He eased from the console, and risked a slow lowering of his arms. 'The ship looked dead. I had no reason to assume anyone was alive. Come to think of it, how *are* you alive? There were no life signs, no energy sources ...

'Shut up.' She waggled the gun. 'Where are you from? Which swallowship, which motherbase?'

'I haven't come from a swallowship. Or a motherbase.' Merlin grimaced. He could see no good way of explaining his situation, or at least none that was likely to improve the mood of this person with the gun. 'I'm what you might call a freelancer. My name is Merlin...'

She cut him off. 'If that's what you're calling yourself, I'd give some serious thought to picking another name.'

'It's worked well enough for me until now.'

'There's only one Merlin. Only one that matters, anyway.'

He gave a self-effacing smile. 'Word got round, then. I suppose it was inevitable, given the time I've been travelling.'

'Word got round, yes. There was a man called Merlin, and he left the Cohort. Shall I tell you what we were taught to think of Merlin?'

'I imagine you're going to.'

'There are two views on him. One is that Merlin was a fool, a self-deluding braggart with an ego to match the size of his delusion.'

'I've never said I was a saint.'

'The other view is that Merlin betrayed the Cohort, that he stole from it and ran from the consequences. That he never had any intention of returning. That he's a liar and criminal and deserves to die for it. So the choice is yours, really. Clown or traitor. Which Merlin are you?'

'Is there a third option?'

'No.' Behind the visor, her eyes narrowed. He could only see the upper part of her face, but it was enough to tell that she was young. 'I don't remember exactly when you ran. But it's been thousands of years, I know that much. You could be anyone. Although why anyone would risk passing themselves off under that name …'

'Then that proves it's me, doesn't it? Only I'd be stupid enough to keep calling myself Merlin.' He tried to appeal to the face. 'It has been thousands of years, but not for me. I've been travelling at near the speed of light for most of that time. *Tyrant* – my ship – is Waynet capable. I've been searching these files …'

'Stealing them.'

'Searching them. I'm deep into territory I don't know well enough to trust, and I thought you might have better charts. You do, as well. But there's something else. Your name, by the way? I mean, since we're having this lovely conversation…'

He read the hesitation in her eyes. A moment when she was on the verge of refusing him even the knowledge of her name, as if she had no intention of him living long enough for it to matter. But something broke and she yielded.

'Teal. And what you mean, something else?'

'In these files. Mention of a syrinx. Is it true? Did you have a syrinx?'

'If your ship is Waynet capable then you already have one.'

Merlin nodded. 'Yes. But mine is damaged, and it doesn't function as well as it used to. I hit a bad kink in the Waynet, and each transition's been harder than the one before. I wasn't expecting to find one here – it was the charts that interested me – but now I know what I've stumbled on…'

'You'll steal it.'

'No. Borrow it, on the implicit understanding that I'm continuing to serve the ultimate good of the Cohort. Teal, you *must* believe me. There's a weapon out there that can shift the balance in this war. To find it I need *Tyrant*, and *Tyrant* needs a syrinx.'

'Then I have some bad news for you. We sold it.' Her tone was off-hand, dismissive. 'It was a double-star system, a few lights back the way we'd come. We needed repairs, material, parts the swallowship couldn't make for itself. We made contact – sent in negotiators. I was on the diplomatic party. We bartered. We left them the syrinx and Pardalote got the things we needed.'

Merlin turned aside in disgust. 'You idiots.'

Teal swiped the barrel of the gun across his faceplate. Merlin flinched back, wondering how close she had been to just shooting him there and then.

'Don't judge us. And don't judge Pardalote for the decisions she took. You weren't there, and you haven't the faintest idea what we went through. Shall I tell you how it was for me?'

Merlin wisely said nothing.

'There's a vault near the middle of the ship,' Teal went on. 'The best place to hide power, if you're going to use it. One by one our frostwatch cabinets failed us. There were a thousand of us, then a hundred... then the last ten. Each time we woke up, counted how many of us were still alive, drew straws to see who got the cabinets that were still working. There were always less and less. I'm the last one, the last of us to get a working cabinet. I ran it on a trickle of power, just the bare minimum. Set the cabinet to wake me if anyone came near.'

Merlin waited a moment then nodded. 'Can I make a suggestion?'

'If it makes you feel better.'

'My ship is warm, it has air, and it's still capable of moving. I feel we'd get to a position of trust a lot quicker if we could speak face to face, without all this glass and vacuum between us.'

He caught her sneer. 'What makes you think I'd ever trust you?'

'People come round to me,' Merlin said.

The syrinx was a matte-black cone about as long as Merlin was tall. It rested in a cradle of metal supports, sharp end pointing aft, in a compartment just forward of *Tyrant*'s engine bay. Syrinxes seemed to work better when they were somewhere close to the centre of mass of a ship, but beyond that there were no clear rules, and much of what *was* known had been pieced together through guesswork and experimentation.

'It still works, to a degree,' Merlin said, stroking a glove along the tapering form. 'But it's dying on me. I daren't say how many more transits I'll get out it.'

'What would you have done if it had failed?' Teal asked, managing to make the question sound peremptory and businesslike, as if she had no real interest in the answer.

They had taken off their helmets, but were still wearing the rest of their suits. Merlin had closed the airlock, but kept *Tyrant* docked with the larger ship. He had shown Teal through the narrow warren of his linked living quarters without stopping to comment, keen to show her that at least the syrinx was a verifiable part of his story.

'I doubt I'd have had much time to worry about it, if it failed. Probably ended up as an interesting smear, that's all.' Merlin offered a smile, but Teal's expression remained hard and unsympathetic.

'A quick death's nothing to complain about.'

She was a hard one for him to fathom. Her head looked too small, too childlike, jutting out from the neck ring of her suit. She was short haired, hard boned, tough and wiry-looking at the same time. He had been right about her eyes, even through the visor. They had seen too much pain and hardship, bottled too much of it inside themselves, and now it was leaking back out.

'You still don't trust me, and that's fine. But let me show you something else.' Merlin beckoned her back through into the living area, then made one of the walls light up with images and maps and text from his private files. The collage was dozens of layers deep, with the records and annotations in just as many languages and alphabets.

'What is this supposed to prove?'

He skimmed rectangles aside, flicking them to the edge of

the wall. Here were Waynet charts, maps of solar systems, schematics of the surfaces of worlds and moons. 'The thing I'm looking for,' he said, 'the weapon, the gun, whatever you want to call it – this is everything that I've managed to find out about it. Clues, rumours, whispers, from a hundred worlds. Maybe they don't all point to the same thing – I'd be amazed if they did. But some of them do, I'm sure of it, and before long I'm going to find the piece that ties the whole thing together.' He stabbed a finger at a nest of numbers next to one of the charts. 'Look how recent these time tags are, Teal. I'm still searching – still gathering evidence.'

Her face was in profile, bathed in the different colours of the images. The slope of her nose, the angle of her chin, reminded him in certain small ways of Sayaca.

She turned to him sharply, as if she had been aware of his gaze.

'I saw pictures of you,' Teal said. 'They showed us them in warcreche. They were a warning against irresponsibility. You look much older than you did in those pictures.'

'Travel broadens the mind. It also puts a large number of lines on you.' He nodded at the collage of records. 'I'm no angel, and I've made mistakes, but this proves I'm still committed. Which means we're both in the same boat, doesn't it? Lone survivors, forced together, each needing to trust the other. Are you really the last of your crew?'

There was a silence before she answered.

'Yes. I knew it before I went under, the last time. There were still others around, but mine was the last reliable cabinet – the only one that stood a chance of working.'

'You were chosen, to have the best chance?'

'Yes.'

He nodded, thinking again of those inner scars. 'Then I've a proposition.' He raised a finger, silencing her before she could get a word out. 'The Huskers did something terrible to you and your people, as they did mine. They deserve to be punished for that, and they will be. Together we can make it happen.'

'By finding your fabled weapon?'

'By finding the syrinx that'll help me carry on with my search. You said that system wasn't far away. If it's on the Waynet, I can reach it in *Tyrant*. We backtrack. If you traded with them once, we can trade again. You've seen that system once before, so you have the local knowledge I most certainly lack.'

She glanced away, her expression clouded by very obvious misgivings.

'We sold them a syrinx,' Teal said. 'One of the rarest, strangest things ever made. All you have is a little black ship and some stories. What could you ever offer them that would be worth that?'

'I'd think of something,' Merlin said.

The transition, when it came, was the hardest so far. Merlin had been expecting the worst and had made sure the two of them were buckled in as tightly as their couches allowed, side by side in *Tyrant*'s command deck. When they slipped into the Waynet it had felt like an impact, a solid scraping blow against the ship, as if it were grinding its way along the flank of an asteroid or iceberg. Alarms sounded, and the hull gave off moans and shrieks of structural complaint. *Tyrant* yawed violently. Probes and stabilisers flaked away from the hull.

But it held. Merlin waited for the instruments to settle down, and for the normal smooth motion of the flow to assert itself. Only then did he start breathing again.

'We're all right. Once we're in the Way, it's rarely too bad. It's just coming in and out that's becoming problematic.' Long experience told him it was safe to unbuckle, and he motioned for Teal to do likewise. She had kept her suit on and her helmet nearby, as if either of those things stood any chance of protecting her if the transition failed completely. Merlin had removed all but the clothes he normally wore in *Tyrant* – baggy and tending to frills and ornamentation.

'How long until we come out again?'

Merlin squinted at one of the indicators. 'About six hours. We're moving very quickly now – only about a hundred billionth part less than the speed of light. Do you see those circles that shoot past us every second?'

They were like the glowing ribs of a tunnel, whisking to either side in an endless, hypnotic procession.

'What are they?'

'Constraining hoops. Anchored back into fixed space. They pin down the Way, keep it flowing in the right direction. In reality, they're about eight light hours apart – far enough that you could easily drop a solar system between them. I think about the Waymakers a lot, you know. They made an empire so old that by the time it fell hardly anyone remembered anything that came before it. Light and wealth and all the sunsets anyone could ever ask for.'

'Look at all the good it did them,' Teal said. 'We're like rats, hunting for crumbs in the ruins they left us.'

'Even rats have their day,' Merlin said. 'And speaking of crumbs… would you like something to eat?'

'What sort of rations do you have?'

He patted his belly. 'We run to a bit more than rations on *Tyrant*.'

With the ship weightless, still rushing down the throat of the Way, they ate with their legs tucked under them in the glass eye of the forward observation bubble. Merlin eyed Teal between mouthfuls, noticing how entirely at ease she was with the absence of gravity, never needing to chase a gobbet of food or a stray blob of water. She had declined his offer of wine, but Merlin saw no need to put himself through such hardship.

'Tell me about the people you traded with,' he said.

'They were fools,' Teal said. She carried on eating for a few mouthfuls. 'But useful fools. They had what we needed, and we had something they considered valuable.'

'Fools, why exactly?'

'They were at war. An interplanetary conflict, fought using fusion ships and fusion bombs. Strategy shaped by artificial intelligences on both sides. It had been going on for centuries when we got there, with only intervals of peace, when the military computers reached a stalemate. Just enough time to rebuild before they started blowing each other to hell again. Two worlds, circling different stars of a binary system, and all the other planets and moons caught up in it in one way or another. A twisted, factional mess. And stupid, too.' She stabbed her fork into the rations as if her meal was something that needed killing. 'Huskers aren't thick in this sector, but you don't go around making noise and light if you've any choice. And there's *always* a choice.'

'We don't seem to have much choice about this war we're in,' Merlin said.

'We're different.' Her eyes were hard and cold. 'This is species-level survival. Their stupid interplanetary war was over trivial ideology. Old grudges, sustained and fanned. Men and women willingly handing their fates to battle computers. Pardalote was reluctant to do business with them: too hard to know who to speak to, who to trust.'

Merlin made a pained, studious look. 'I'd never meddle in someone else's war.'

She pushed the fork around. 'In the end it wasn't too bad. We identified the side best placed to help us, and got in and out before there were too many complications.'

'Complications?'

'There weren't any. Not in the end.' She was silent for a second or two. 'I was glad to leave that stupid place. I've barely thought about them since.'

'Your logs say you were in that system thirteen hundred years ago. A lot could have changed since then. Who knows, maybe they've patched up their differences.'

'And maybe the Huskers found them.'

'You know what, Teal? You're cheerful company.'

'Seeing the rest of your crew die will do that. You chose to leave, Merlin – it wasn't that you were the last survivor.'

He sipped at his wine, debating how much of a clear head he would need when they emerged from the Way. Sometimes a clear head was the last thing that helped.

'I lost good people as well, Teal.'

'Really?'

He pushed off, moved to a cabinet and drew out a pair of immersion suits.

'If you went through warcreche you'll know what these are. Do you trust me enough to put one on?'

Teal took the dun-coloured garment and studied it with unveiled distaste. 'What good will this do?'

'Put it on. I want to show you what I lost.'

'We'll win this war in reality, not simulations. There's nothing you can show me that …'

'Just do it, Teal.'

She scowled at him, but went into a back room of *Tyrant* to remove her own clothes and don the tight-fitting immersion suit. By the time she was ready Merlin had slipped into the other suit. He nodded at Teal as she spidered back into the cabin. 'Good. Trust is good. We'll only be inside a little while, but I think it'll help. Ship, patch us through.'

'The Palace, Merlin?'

'Where else?'

The suit prickled his neck as it established its connection with his spine. There was the usual moment of dislocation and *Tyrant* melted away, to be replaced by a surrounding of warm stone walls and tall fretted windows, shot through with amber sun.

Teal was standing next to him.

'Where are we?'

'Where I was born. Where my brother and I spent the first couple of decades of our existence, before the Cohort came.' Merlin walked to the nearest window and bid Teal to follow him.

'Gallinule created this environment long after we left. He's gone now as well, so this is a reminder of the past for me in more ways than one.'

'Your brother's dead?'

'It's complicated.'

She left it at that. 'What world are we on?'

'Plenitude, we called it. Common enough name, I suppose.' Merlin stepped onto a plinth under the window, offering a better view through its fretwork. 'Do you see the land below?'

Teal strained to look down. 'It's moving – sliding under us. I thought we were in a castle or something.'

'We are. The Palace of Eternal Dusk. My family home for thirteen hundred years – as long as the interval between your visits to that system.' He touched his hand against the stonework. 'We didn't make this place. It was unoccupied for centuries, circling Plenitude at exactly the same speed as the line between day and night. My family were the first to reach it from the surface, using supersonic aircraft. We held it for the next forty generations.' He lifted his face to the unchanging aspect of the sun, hovering at its fixed position over the endlessly flowing horizon. 'My uncle was a bit of an amateur archaeologist. He dug deep into the rock the palace is built on, as far down as the anti-gravity keel. He said he found evidence that it was at least twenty thousand years old, and maybe quite a bit more than that.' Merlin touched a hand to Teal's shoulder. 'Let me show you something else.'

She flinched under his touch but allowed him to steer her to one of the parlours branching off the main room. Merlin halted them both at the door, touching a finger to his lips. Two boys knelt on a carpet in the middle of the parlour, their forms side-lit by golden light. They were surrounded by toy armies, spread out in ordered regiments and platoons.

'Gallinule and I,' Merlin whispered, as the younger of the boys took his turn to move a mounted and penanted figure from one flank to another. 'Dreaming of war. Little did we know we'd get more than our share of it.'

He backed away, leaving the boys to their games, and took Teal to the next parlour.

Here an old woman sat in a stern black chair, facing one of the sunlit windows with her face mostly averted from the door. She wore black and had her hands in her lap, keeping perfectly still and watchful.

'Years later,' Merlin said, 'Gallinule and I were taken from Plenitude. It was meant to be an act of kindness, preserving something of our world in advance of the Huskers. But it tore us from our mother. We couldn't return to her. She was left here with the ruins of empire, her sons gone, her world soon to fall.'

The woman seemed aware of her visitors. She turned slightly, bringing more of her face into view. Her eyes searched the door, as if looking for ghosts.

'She has a gentle look,' Teal said quietly.

'She was kind,' Merlin answered softly. 'They spoke ill of her, but they didn't know her, not the way Gallinule and I did.'

The woman slowly turned back to face the window. Her face was in profile again, her eyes glistening.

'Does she ever speak?'

'She's no cause to.' Merlin's mouth was dry for a few moments. 'We saw it happen, from the swallowship. Saw the Husker weapons strike Plenitude – saw the fall of the Palace of Eternal Dusk.' Merlin turned from the tableau of his mother. 'I mean to go back, one of these days – see what's left with my own eyes. But I find it hard to bring myself to.'

'How many died?' Teal asked.

'Hundreds of millions. We were the only two that Quail managed to save, along with a few fragments of cultural knowledge. So I know what it's like, Teal – believe me I know what it's like.' He turned from her with a cold disregard. 'Ship, bring Teal out.'

'What about you?'

'I need a little time on my own. You can start remembering

21

everything I need to know about the binary system. You've got about five hours.'

Tyrant pulled Teal out of the Palace. Merlin stood alone, silent, for long moments. Then he returned to the parlour where his mother watched the window, imprisoned in an endless golden day, and he stood in her shadow wondering what it would take to free her from that reverie of loss and loneliness.

They made a safe emergence from the Waynet, Merlin holding his breath until they were out and stable and the syrinx had stopped ringing in its cradle like a badly-cracked bell.

He took a few minutes to assess their surroundings.

Two stars, close enough together for fusion ships to make a crossing between them in weeks. A dozen large worlds, scattered evenly between the two stars. Hundreds of moons and minor bodies. Thousands of moving ships, easily tracked across interplanetary distance, the vessels grouped into squadrons and attack formations. Battle stations and super-carriers. Fortresses and cordons. The occasional flash of a nuclear weapon or energy pulse weapon – battle ongoing.

Tyrant was stealthy, but even a stealthy ship made a big splash coming out of the Waynet. Merlin wasn't at all surprised when a large vessel locked onto them and closed in fast, presumably pushing its fusion engines to the limit.

Teal carried on briefing him as the ship approached.

'I don't like the look of that thing,' *Tyrant* said, as soon as they had a clear view.

'I don't either,' Merlin said. 'We'll treat it respectfully. Wouldn't want you getting a scratch on your paintwork, would we?'

The vessel was three times as large as Merlin's ship and every inch a thing of war. Guns bristled from its hull. It was made of old alloys, forged and joined by venerable methods, and its engines and weapons depended on the antique alchemy of magnetically bottled fusion. A snarling mouth that had been painted across the front of the ship, crammed with razor-tipped teeth.

'It's a Havergal ship,' Teal said. 'That's their marking, that dagger-and-star. It doesn't look all that different to the ships they had when we were here before.'

'Fusion's a plateau technology,' Merlin remarked. 'If all they ever needed to do was get around this binary system and blow each other up now and then, it would have been sufficient.'

'They knew about the Waynet, of course – hard to miss it, cutting through their sky the way it does. That interested them. They wanted to jump all the way from fusion to syrinx technology, without all the hard stuff in between.'

'Doesn't look like they got very far, does it?'

The angry-looking ship drew alongside. An airlock opened and a squad of armoured figures came out on rocket packs. Merlin remained tense, but commanded *Tyrant's* weapons to remain inside their hatches. He also told the proctors to hide themselves away until he needed them.

Footfalls clanged onto the hull. Grappling devices slid like nails on rust. Merlin opened his airlock, nodded at Teal, and the two of them went to meet the boarding party. He was half way there when a thought occurred to him. 'Unless they bring up your earlier visit, don't mention it. You're just along for the ride with me. I want to know if there's anything they say or do that doesn't fit with your picture of them – anything they might be keeping from me.'

'I speak their language. Isn't that going to take some explaining?'

'Feign ignorance to start with, then make it seem as if you're picking it up as you go. If they get suspicious, we'll just say that there are a dozen other systems in this sector where they speak a similar dialect.' He flashed a nervous smile at Teal. 'Or something. Make it up. Be creative.'

The airlock had cycled by the time they arrived. When it

opened, Merlin was not surprised to find only two members of the boarding party inside. There would not have been room for more.

'Welcome,' he said, making a flourishing gesture of invitation. 'Come in, come in. Take your shoes off. Make yourselves at home.'

They were a formidable looking pair. Their vacuum armour had a martial look to it, with bladed edges and spurs, a kind of stabbing ram on the crowns of their helmets, fierce-looking grills across the glass of their faceplates. All manner of guns and close-combat weapons buckled or braced to the armour. The armour was green, with gold ornamentation.

Merlin tapped his throat. 'Take your helmets off. The worst you'll catch is a sniffle.'

They came into the ship. Their faces were lost behind the grills, but he caught the movement as they twisted to look at each other, before reaching up to undo their helmets. They came free with a tremendous huff of equalising pressure, revealing a pair of heads. There were two men, both bald, with multiple blemishes and battle-scars across their scalps. They had tough, grizzled-looking features, with lantern jaws and a dusting of dark stubble across their chins and cheeks. A duelling scar or similar across the face of one man, a laser burn ruining the ear of the other. Their small, cold-seeming eyes were pushed back into a sea of wrinkles. One man opened his mouth, revealing a cage of yellow and metal teeth.

He barked out something, barely a syllable. His voice was very deep, and Merlin caught a blast of stale breath as he spoke. The other man waited a moment then amplified this demand or greeting with a few more syllables of his own.

Merlin returned these statements with an uneasy smile of his own. 'I'm Merlin,' he said. 'And I come in peace. Ish.'

'They don't understand you,' Teal whispered.

'I'm damned glad they don't. Did you get anything of what they said?'

'They want to know why you're here and what you want.'

The first man said a few more words, still in the same angry, forceful tone as before. The second man glanced around and touched one of the control panels next to the airlock.

'Isn't war lovely,' Merlin said.

'I understand them,' Teal said, still in a whisper. 'Well enough, anyway. They're still using the main Havergal language. It's shifted a bit, but I can still get the gist. How much do you want me to pretend to understand?'

'Nothing yet. Keep soaking it in. When you think you've given it long enough, point to the two of us and make the sound for "friend".' Merlin grinned back at the suited men, the two of them edging away from the lock in opposite directions. 'I know; it needs a little work, doesn't it? Tired décor. I'm thinking of knocking out this wall, maybe putting a window in over there?'

Teal said something, jabbing one hand at her chest and another at Merlin. 'Friendly,' she said. 'I've told them we're friendly. What else?'

'Give them our names. Then tell them we'd like to speak to whoever's in charge of that planet you mentioned.'

He caught "Merlin" and "Teal" and the name "Havergal". He had to trust that she was doing a good job of making her initial efforts seem plausibly imperfect, even as she stumbled into ever-improving fluency. Whatever she had said, though, it had a sudden and visible effect. The crag-faced men came closer together again and now directed their utterances at Teal alone, guessing that was the only one who had any kind of knowledge of their language.

'What?' Merlin asked.

'They're puzzled that I speak their tongue. They also want to know if you have a syrinx.'

'Tell them I have a syrinx but that it doesn't work very well.' Merlin was still smiling at the men, but the muscles around his mouth were starting to ache. 'And tell them I apologise for not speaking their tongue, but you're much better at languages than me. What are their names, too?'

'I'll ask.' There was another halting exchange, Merlin sensing that the names were given grudgingly, but she drew them out in the end. 'Balus,' Teal said. 'And Locrian. I'd tell you which is which, but I'm not sure there'd be much point.'

'Good. Thank Balus and Locrian for the friendly reception. Tell them that they are very welcome on my ship, but I'd be very obliged if the others stopped crawling around outside my hull.' Merlin paused. 'Oh, and one other thing. Ask them if they're still at war with Gaffurius.'

He had no need of Teal to translate the answer to that particular part of his query. Balus – or perhaps Locrian – made a hawking sound, as if he meant to spit. Merlin was glad that he did not deliver on the gesture; the intention had been transparent enough.

'He says,' Teal replied, 'that the Gaffurians broke the terms of the recent treaty. And the one before that. And the one before that. He said the Gaffurians have the blood of pigs in their veins. He also says that he would rather cut out his own tongue than speak of the Gaffurians in polite company.'

'One or two bridges to build there, then.'

'He also asks why they should care what you think of the ones still on your hull.'

'It's a fair question. How good do you think you're getting with this language of theirs?'

'Better than I'm letting on.'

'Well, let's push our luck a little. Tell Balus – or Locrian – that I have weapons on this ship. Big, dangerous weapons. Weapons neither of them will have ever seen before. Weapons that – if they understood their potency, and how near they've allowed that ship of theirs to come – would make them empty their bowels so quickly they'd fill their own spacesuits up to the neck ring. Can you do that for me?'

'How about I tell them that you're armed, that you're ready to defend your property, but that you still want to proceed from a position of peaceful negotiation?'

'On balance, probably for the best.'

'I'll also add that you've come to find out about a syrinx, and you're prepared to discuss terms of trade.'

'Do that.'

Merlin waited while this laborious exchange was carried on. Teal reached some sort of critical juncture in her statement and this drew a renewed burst of angry exclamations from Balus and Locrian – he guessed they had just been acquainted with the notion that *Tyrant* was armed – but Teal continued and her words appeared to have some temporary soothing effect, or as best as could be expected. Merlin raised his hands in his best placating manner. 'Honestly, I'm not the hair-trigger type. We just need to have a basis for mutual respect here.'

'Cohort?' he heard one of them say.

'Yes,' he answered, at the same time as Teal. 'Cohort. Big bad Cohort.'

After a great deal of to-ing and fro-ing, Teal turned to him: 'They don't claim to know anything about a syrinx. Then again, I don't think these men necessarily *would* know. But one of them, Locrian, is going back to the other ship. I think he needs to signal some higher-up or something.'

'It's what I was expecting,' Merlin said. 'Tell him I'll wait. And tell the other one he's welcome to drink with us.'

Teal relayed this message, then said: 'He'll stay, but he doesn't need anything to drink.

'His loss.'

While Locrian went back through the airlock, Balus joined them in the lounge, looking incongruous in his heavily-armoured suit. Teal tried to engage him in conversation, but he had obviously been ordered to keep his communications to a strict minimum. Merlin helped himself to some wine, before catching his own pink-eyed reflection and deciding enough was enough, for now.

'What do you think's going on?' Teal asked, when an hour

had passed with no word from the other ship.

'Stuff.'

'Aren't you concerned?'

'Terribly.'

'You don't look or sound it. You want this syrinx, don't you?'

'Very much so.'

Balus looked on silently as his hosts spoke in Main. If he understood any part of it, there was no clue on his face. 'But you seem so nonchalant about it all,' Teal said.

Merlin pondered this for a few seconds. 'Do you think being *not* nonchalant would make any difference? I don't know that it would. We're here in the moment, aren't we? And the moment will have its way with us, no matter how we feel about things.'

'Fatalist.'

'Cheerful realist. There's a distinction.' Merlin raised his empty, wine-stained glass. 'Isn't there, Balus? You agree, don't you, my fine fellow?'

Balus parted his lips and gave a grunt.

'They're coming back,' Teal said, catching movement through the nearest window. 'A shuttle of some sort, not just people in suits. Is that good or bad?'

'We'll find out.' Merlin bristled a hand across his chin. 'Mind me while I go and shave my beard.'

'Shave your tongue while you're at it.'

Merlin had just finished freshening up when the lock completed its cycle and the two suited individuals came aboard. One of them, wearing a green and gold suit, turned out to be Locrian. He took off his helmet and motioned for the other, wearing a red and gold suit, to do likewise. This suit was less ostentatiously armoured than the other, designed for a smaller frame. But when the figure lifted their helmet off, glanced at Locrian and uttered a few terse words, Merlin had no difficulty picking up on the power relationship between the two.

The newcomer was an old man – old, at least, in Merlin's

reckoning. Seventy or eighty years, by the Cohort way of accounting such things. He had fine, aristocratic features, accented by a high, imperious brow and a back-combed sweep of pure white hair. His eyes were a liquid grey, like little wells of mercury, suggesting a sharp, relentless intelligence.

Officer class, Merlin thought.

The man spoke to them. His voice was soft, undemonstrative. Merlin still did not understand a word of it, but just the manner of speaking conveyed an assumption of implicit authority.

'His name is ... Baskin,' Teal said, when the man had left a silence for her to speak. 'Prince Baskin. Havergal royalty. That's his own personal cruiser out there. He was on some sort of patrol when they picked up our presence. They came at full thrust to meet us. Baskin says things come out of the Way now and then, and it's always a scramble to get to them before the enemy.'

'If Locrian's spoken to him, then he already knows our names. Ask him about the syrinx.'

Teal passed on Merlin's question. Baskin answered, Teal ruminated on his words, then said: 'He says that he's very interested to learn of your interest in the syrinx.'

'I bet he is.'

'He also says that he'd like to continue the conversation on his cruiser. He says that we'll be guests, not prisoners, and that we'll be free to return here whenever we like.'

'Tell Prince Baskin ... yes, we'll join him. But if I'm not back on *Tyrant* in twelve hours, my ship will take action to retrieve me. If you can make that sound like a polite statement of fact, rather than a crudely-worded threat, that would be lovely.'

'He says there'll be no difficulty,' Teal said.

'He's right about that,' Merlin answered.

Part of Prince Baskin's cruiser had been spun to simulate gravity. There was a stateroom, as grand as anything Merlin had encountered, all shades of veneered wood and polished metal, with red drapes and red fabric on the chairs. The floor curved up gently from one end of the room to the other, and this curvature was echoed in the grand table that took up much of the space. Prince Baskin was at one end of it, Merlin and Teal at the other, with the angle of the floor making Baskin seem to tilt forward like a playing card, having to lift his head to face his guests. Orderlies had fussed around them for some time, setting plates and glasses and cutlery, before bringing in the elements of a simple but well-prepared meal. Then – rather to Merlin's surprise – they had left the three of them alone, with only stony-faced portraits of royal ancestors and nobility for company. Men on horses, men in armour, men with projectile guns and energy weapons, both grand and foolish in their pomp.

'This is pure ostentation,' he said, looking around the room with its sweeping curves and odd angles. 'No one in their right mind puts centrifugal gravity on a ship this small. It takes up too much room, costs too much in mass, and the spin differential between your feet and head's enough to make you dizzy.'

'If the surroundings are not quite to your taste, Merlin, we could adjourn to one of the *Renouncer*'s weightless areas.'

Prince Baskin had spoken.

Teal cocked her chin to face him. The curvature of the room made it like talking to someone half way up a hill. 'You speak Main.'

'I try.'

'Then why ...' she began.

Baskin smiled, and tore a chunk off some bread, dipping it into soup before proceeding. 'Please join me. And please forgive my slight deception in pretending to need to have your words translated, as well as my rustiness with your tongue. What I have learned, I have done so from books and recordings, and until now I have never had the opportunity to speak it to a living soul.' He bit into the bread, and made an eager motioning gesture that they should do likewise. 'Please. Eat. My cook is excellent – as well he should be, given what it costs me to ship him and his kitchen around. Teal, I *must* apologise. But there was no deception where Locrian and Balus were concerned. They genuinely did not speak Main, and were in need of your translation. I am very much the exception.'

'How ...' Merlin started.

'I was a sickly child, I suppose you might say. I had many hours to myself, and in those hours – as one does – I sought my own entertainment. I used to play at war, but toy soldiers and tabletop campaigns will only take you so far. So I developed a fascination with languages. Many centuries ago, a Cohort ship stopped in our system. They were here for two years – two of *your* years, I should say - long enough for trade and communication. Our diplomats tried to learn Main, and by the same token the Cohort sent in negotiating teams who did their best to master our language. Of course there were linguistic ties between the two, so the task was not insurmountable. But difficult, all the same. I doubt that either party excelled itself, but we did what was needed and there was sufficient mutual understanding.' Baskin turned his head to glance at the portraits to his right, each painting set at a slight angle to its neighbours. 'It *was* a very long time ago, as I'm sure you appreciate. When the Cohort had gone, there was great emphasis placed on maintaining our grasp of their language, so that we'd have a head start the next time we needed it. Schools, academies, and so on. King Curtal was instrumental in that.' He was nodding at one of the figures in the portraits, a man of similar age and bearing to himself, and dressed in state finery not too far removed from the formal wear in which Baskin now appeared. 'But that soon died away. The Cohort never returned and, as the centuries passed, there was less and less enthusiasm for learning Main. The schools closed, and by the time it came down to me – forty generations later – all that remained were the books and recordings. There was no living speaker of Main. So I set myself the challenge to become one, and encouraged my senior staff to do likewise, and here I am now, sitting before you, and doubtless making a grotesque mockery of your tongue.'

Merlin broke bread, dipped it into the soup, made a show of chewing on it before answering.

'This Cohort ship that dropped by,' he said, his mouth still full. 'Was it the *Shrike*?'

Teal held her composure, but he caught the sidelong twitch of her eye.

'Yes,' Baskin said, grimacing slightly. 'You've heard of it?'

'It's how I know about the syrinx,' Merlin said, trying to sound effortlessly matter-of-fact. 'I found the *Shrike*. It was a wreck, all her crew dead. Been dead for centuries, in fact. But the computer records were still intact.' He lifted a goblet and drank. The local equivalent to wine was amber coloured and had a lingering, woody finish. Not exactly to his taste but he'd had worse. 'That's why I'm here.'

'And Teal?'

'I travel with Merlin,' she said. 'He isn't good with languages, and he pays me to be his translator.'

'You showed a surprising faculty with our own,' Baskin said.

'Records of your language were in the files Merlin pulled from the wreck. It wasn't that hard to pick up the rudiments.'

Baskin dabbed at his chin with napkin. 'You picked up more than the rudiments, if I might say.'

Merlin leaned forward. 'Is it true about the syrinx?'

'Yes,' Baskin said. 'We keep it in a safe place on Havergal. Intact, in so far as we can tell. Would that be of interest to you?'

'I think it might.'

'But you must already have one, if you've come here by the Way.'

Teal said: 'His syrinx is broken, or at least damaged. He knows it won't last long, so he needs to find a spare.'

Again Baskin turned to survey the line of portraits. 'These ancestors of mine knew very little but war. It dominated their lives utterly. Even when there was peace, they were thinking ahead to the moment that peace would fail, and how they might be in the most advantageous position when that day came. As it always did. My own life has also been shaped by the war. Disfigured, you might say. But I have lived under its shadow long enough. I should very much like to be the last of my line who ruled during wartime.'

'Then end the war,' Merlin said.

'I should like to – but it must be under our terms. Gaffurius is stretched to its limits. One last push, one last offensive, and we can enforce a lasting peace. But there is a difficulty.'

'Which is?' Teal asked.

'Something of ours has fallen into the wrong hands – an object we call the Iron Tactician.' Baskin continued eating for several moments, in no rush to explain himself. 'I don't know what you've learned of our history. But for centuries, both sides in this war have relied on artificial intelligences to guide their military planning.'

'I suppose this is another of those machines,' Merlin said.

'Yes and no. For a long time our machines were well-matched with those of the enemy. We would build a better one, then they would, we would respond, and so on. A gradual escalating improvement. So it went on. Then – by some happy stroke – our cyberneticists created a machine that was generations in advance of anything they had. For fifty years the Iron Tactician has given us an edge, a superiority. Its forecasts are seldom in error. The enemy still has nothing to match it – which is why we have made the gains that we have. But now, on the eve of triumph, we have lost the Iron Tactician.'

'Careless,' Merlin said.

A tightness pinched the corner of Baskin's mouth. 'The Tactician has always needed to be close to the theatre of battle, so that its input data is as accurate and up-to-date as possible. That was why our technicians made it portable, self-contained and self-reliant. Of course there are risks in having an asset of that nature.'

'What happened?' Teal asked. 'Did Gaffurius capture it?'

'Thankfully, no,' Baskin answered. 'But it's very nearly as bad. The Tactician has fallen into the hands of a non-aligned third party. Brigands, mercenaries, call them what you will. Now they wish to extract a ransom for the Tactician's safe return – or they will sell it on to the enemy. We know their location, an asteroid holdout, and if we massed a group of ships we could probably overwhelm their defences. But if Gaffurius guessed our intentions and moved first ...' Baskin lifted his glass, peering through it at Merlin and Teal, so that his face swam distorted, one mercurial eye wobbling to immensity while the other shrunk to a tight cold glint. 'So there you have it. A simple proposition. The syrinx is yours, Merlin – provided you recover the Tactician for us.'

'Maybe I still wouldn't be fast enough.'

'But you'll be able to strike without warning, with Cohort weapons. I don't see that it should pose you any great difficulty, given the evident capabilities of your ship.' Baskin twirled his fingers around the stem of his goblet. 'But then that depends on how badly you want our syrinx.'

'Mm,' Merlin said. 'Quite badly, if I'm going to be honest.'

'Would you do it?'

Merlin looked at Teal before answering. But she seemed distracted, her gaze caught by one of the portraits. It was the picture of King Curtal, the ancestor Baskin had mentioned only a little while earlier. While the style of dress might not have changed, the portrait was yellowing with old varnish, its colours time-muted.

'I'd need guarantees,' he said. 'Starting with proof that this syrinx even exists.'

'That's easily arranged,' Prince Baskin said.

Tyrant had a biometric lock on Merlin, and it would shadow the *Renouncer* all the way to Havergal. If it detected that Merlin was injured or under duress, *Tyrant* would deploy its own proctors to storm the cruiser. But Merlin had gauged enough of his hosts to conclude that such an outcome was vanishingly unlikely. They needed his cooperation much too badly to do harm to their guest.

Locrian showed Merlin and Teal to their quarters, furnished in the same sumptuous tones as the stateroom. When the door opened and Merlin saw that there was only one bed, albeit a large one, he turned to Teal with faked resignation.

'It's awkward for both of us, but if we want to keep them thinking you've been travelling with me for years and years, it'll help if we behave as a couple.'

Teal waited until Locrian had shut the door on them and gone off on his own business. She walked to the bed, following the gently, dreamy up-curve of the floor. 'You're right,' she said, glancing back at Merlin before she sat on the edge of the bed. 'It will help. And at least for now I'd rather they didn't know I was on the swallowship, so I'm keen to maintain the lie.'

'Good. Very good.'

'But we share the bed and nothing else. You're of no interest to me, Merlin. Maybe you're not a traitor or a fool – I'll give you that much. But you're still a fat, swaggering drunk who thinks far too much of himself.' But Teal patted the bed. 'Still, you're right. The illusion's useful.'

Merlin settled himself down on his side of the bed. 'No room for manoeuvre there? Not even a little bit?'

'None.'

'Then we're clear. Actually, it's a bit of a relief. I meant to say...'

'If this is about what I just spoke about?'

'I just wanted to say, I understand how strange all this must be. Not everyone goes back to a place they were thirteen hundred years ago. In a way, it's a good job it was such a long time ago. At least we don't have to contend with any living survivors from those days, saying that they remember you being on the diplomatic team.'

'It was forty three generations ago. No one remembers.'

Merlin moved to the window, watching the stars wheel slowly by outside. There was his own ship, a sharp sliver of darkness against the greater darkness of space. He thought of the loves he had seen ripped from by time and distance, and how the sting of those losses grew duller with each year but was never entirely healed. It was an old lesson for him, one he had been forced to learn many times. For Teal, this might be her first real taste of the cruelty of deep time – realising how far downstream she had come, how little chance she stood of beating those currents back to better, kinder times.

'I'd remember,' he said softly.

He could see her reflection in the window, *Tyrant* sliding through her like a barb, but Teal neither acknowledged his words nor showed the least sign that they had meant anything to her.

Five days was indeed ample time to prepare Merlin for the recovery operation, but only because the intelligence was so sparse. The brigands were holed up on an asteroid called Mundar, an otherwise insignificant speck of dirt on some complex, winding orbit that brought it into the territorial space of both Havergal and Gaffurius. Their leader was a man called Struxer, but beyond one fuzzy picture the biographical notes were sparse. Fortunately there was more on the computer itself. The Iron Tactician was a spherical object about four metres across, quilted from pole to pole in thick military-grade armour. It looked like some hard-shelled animal rolled up into a defensive ball. Merlin saw no obvious complications: it needed no external power inputs and would easily fit within *Tyrant*'s cargo hold.

Getting hold of it was another matter. Baskin's military staff knew how big Mundar was and had estimates of its fortifications, but beyond that things were sketchy. Merlin skimmed the diagrams and translated documents, but told Baskin that he wanted Teal to see the originals. He was still looking out for any gaps between the raw material and what was deemed fit for his eyes, any hint of a cover-up or obfuscation.

'Why are you so concerned?' Teal asked him, halfway to Havergal, when they were alone in Baskin's stateroom, the documents spread out on the table. 'Eating away at your conscience, is it, that you might be serving the wrong paymasters?'

'I'm not the one who chose sides,' he said quietly. 'You did, by selling the syrinx to one party instead of the other. Besides, the other lot won't be any better. Just a different bunch of stuffed shirts and titles, being told what to do by a different bunch of battle computers.'

'So you've no qualms.'

'Qualms?' Merlin set down the papers he had been leafing through. 'I've so many qualms they're in danger of self-organizing. I occasionally have a thought that *isn't* a qualm. But I'll tell you this. Sometimes you just have to do the obvious thing. They have an item I need, and there's a favour I can do for them. It's that simple. Not everything in the universe is a riddle.'

'You'll be killing those brigands.'

'They'll have every chance to hand over the goods. And I'll exercise due restraint. I don't want to damage the Tactician, not when it's the only thing standing between me and the syrinx.'

'What if you found out that Prince Baskin was a bloodthirsty warmonger?'

Merlin, suddenly weary, settled his head onto his hand, propped up with an elbow. 'Shall I tell you something? This war of theirs doesn't matter. I don't give a damn who wins or who loses, or how many lives end up being lost because of it. What matters – what *my* problem is – is the simple fact that the Huskers will wipe out every living trace of humanity if we allow them. That includes you, me, Prince Baskin, Struxer's brigands, and every human being on either side of their little spat. And if a few people end up dying to make that Husker annihilation a little less likely, a few stupid mercenaries who should have known better than to play one side against the other, I'm afraid I'm not going to shed many tears.'

'You're cold.'

'No one loves life more than me, Teal. No one's lost more, either. You lost a ship, and that's bad, but I lost a whole world. And regardless of which side they're on, these people will all die if I don't act.' He returned to the papers, with their sketchy ideas about Mundar's reinforcements, but whatever focus he'd had was gone now. 'They owe you nothing, Teal, and you owe them nothing in return. The fact that you were here all those years ago... it doesn't matter. Nothing came of it.'

Teal was silent. He thought that was going to be the end of it, that his words had found their mark, but after a few moments she said: 'Something isn't right. The man in the portrait – the one they call King Curtal. I knew him. But that wasn't his name.'

As they made their approach to Havergal, slipping through cordon after cordon of patrols and defence stations, between armoured moons and belts of anti-ship mines, dodging patrol zones and battle fronts, Merlin felt a sickness building in him. He had seen worse things done to worlds in his travels. Much worse, in many cases: seen worlds reduced to molten slag or tumbling rubble piles or clouds of hot, chemically complex dust. But with few exceptions those horrors had been perpetrated not by people but by forces utterly beyond their control or comprehension. Not so here. The boiled oceans, the cratered landmasses, the dead and ashen forests, the poisoned, choking remnants of what had once been a life-giving atmosphere – these brutalities had been perpetrated by human action, people against people. It was an unnecessary and wanton crime, a cruel and injudicious act in a galaxy that already knew more than its share.

'Is Gaffurius like this?' Merlin asked, as *Renouncer* cleaved its way to ground, *Tyrant* matching its course with an effortless insouciance.

'Gaffurius?' Baskin asked, a fan of wrinkles appearing at the corner of his eyes. 'No, much, much worse. At least we still have a few surface settlements, a few areas where the atmosphere is still breathable.'

'I wouldn't count that as too much of a triumph.' Merlin's mind was flashing back to the last days of Lecythus, the tainted rubble of its shattered cities, the grey heave of its restless cold ocean, waiting to reclaim what humans had left to ruin. He remembered Minla taking him to the huge whetstone monument, the edifice upon which she had embossed the version of events she wished to be codified as historical truth, long after she and her government were dust.

'Don't judge us too harshly, Merlin,' Baskin said. 'We don't choose to be enmeshed in this war.'

'Then end it.'

'I intend to. But would you opt for any ceasefire with the Huskers, irrespective of the terms?' He looked at Merlin, then at Teal, the three of them in *Renouncer*'s sweeping command bridge, standing before its wide arc of windows, shuttered for the moment against the glare of re-entry. Of course you wouldn't. War is a terrible thing. But there are kinds of peace that are worse.'

'I haven't seen much evidence of that,' Merlin said.

'Oh, come now. Two men don't have to spend too much time in each other's company to know each other for what they are. We're not so different, Merlin. We disdain war, affect a revulsion for it, but deep down it'll always be in our blood. Without it, we wouldn't know what to do with ourselves.'

Teal spoke up. 'When we first met, Prince Baskin, you mentioned that you hadn't always had this interest in languages. What was it you said? Toy soldiers and campaigns will only get you so far? That you used to play at war?'

'In your language – in Main,' Baskin said, 'the word for school is "warcreche". You learn war from the moment you can toddle.'

'But we don't play at it,' Teal said.

The two ships shook off their cocoons of plasma and bellied into the thicker airs near the surface. They levelled into horizontal flight, and the windows de-shuttered themselves, Merlin blinking against the sudden silvery brightness of day. They were overflying a ravaged landscape, pressed beneath a low, oppressive cloud ceiling. Merlin searched the rolling terrain for evidence of a single living thing, but all he saw was desolation. Here and there was the faint scratch of what might once have been a road, or the gridded thumbprint of some former town, but it was clear that no one now lived among these ruins. Ravines, deep and ominous, sliced their way through the abandoned roads. There were so many craters, their walls interlacing, that it was as if rain had begun to fall on some dull grey lake, creating a momentary pattern of interlinked ripples.

'If I need a planet looking after,' Merlin mumbled, 'remind me not to trust it to any of you lot.'

'We'll rebuild,' Baskin said, setting his hands on the rail that ran under the sweep of windows. 'Reclaim. Cleanse and resettle. Even now our genetic engineers are designing the hardy plant species that will re-blanket these lands in green and start making our atmosphere fit for human lungs.' He caught himself, offering a self-critical smile. 'You'll forgive me. Too easy to forget that I'm not making some morale-boosting speech at one of our armaments complexes.'

'Where do you all live now?' Teal asked. 'There were surface cities here once… weren't there?'

'We abandoned the last of those cities, Lurga, when I was just out of boyhood,' Baskin said. 'Now we live in underground communities, impervious to nuclear assault.'

'I bet the views are just splendid,' Merlin said.

Baskin met his sarcasm with a grim absence of humour. 'We endure, Merlin – as the Cohort endures. Here. We're approaching the entry duct to one of the sub-cities. Do you see that sloping hole?' He was nodding at an angled mouth, jutting from the ground like a python buried up to its eyes. 'The Gaffurians are good at destruction, but less good at precision. They can impair our moons and asteroids, but their weapons haven't the accuracy to strike across space and find a target that small. We'll return, a little later, and you'll be made very welcome. But first I'd like to settle any doubts you might have about the syrinx. We'll continue a little way north, into the highlands. I promise it won't take long.'

Baskin was true to his word, and they had only flown for a few more minutes when the terrain began to buckle and wrinkle into the beginnings of a barren, treeless mountain range, rising in a series of forbidding steps until even the high-flying spacecraft were forced to increase their altitude. 'Most of our military production takes place in these upland sectors,' Baskin said. 'We have ready access to metallic ores, heavy isotopes, geothermal energy and so on. Of course it's well guarded. Missile and particle beams will be locking onto us routinely, both our ships. The only thing preventing either of them being shot down is our imperial authorisation.'

'That and the countermeasures on my ship,' Merlin said. 'Which could peel back these mountains like a scab, if they detected a threat worth bothering with.'

But in truth he felt vulnerable and was prepared to admit it, if only to himself. He could feel the nervous, bristling presence of all that unseen weaponry, like a migraine under the skin of Havergal.

Soon another mouth presented itself. It was wedged at the base of an almost sheer-sided valley.

'Prepare for descent,' Baskin said. 'It'll be a tight squeeze, but your ship shouldn't have any difficulties following.'

They dived into the mouth and went deep. Kilometres, and then tens of kilometres, before swerving sharply into a horizontal shaft. Merlin allowed not a flicker of a reaction to betray his feelings, but the fact was that he was impressed, in a grudging, disapproving way. There was expertise and determination here – qualities that the Cohort's military engineers could well have appreciated. Anyone who could dig tunnels was handy in a war.

A glowing orange light shone ahead. Merlin was just starting to puzzle over its origin when they burst into a huge underground chamber, a bubble in the crust of Havergal. The floor of the bubble was a sea of lava, spitting and churning, turbulent with the eddies and currents of some mighty underground flow which just happened to pass in and out of this chamber. Suspended in the middle of the rocky void, underlit by flickering orange light, was a dark structure shaped like an inverted cone, braced in a ring and attached to the chamber's walls by three skeletal, cantilevered arms. It was the size of a small palace or space station, and its flattened upper surface was easily spacious enough for both ships to set down on with room to spare.

Bulkily suited figures – presumably protected against the heat and toxic airs of this place – came out and circled the ships. They attached a flexible docking connection to *Renouncer*.

'We call it the facility,' Baskin said, as he and his guests walked down the sloping throat of the docking connector. 'Just that. No capital letters, nothing to suggest its ultimate importance. But for many centuries this was the single most important element in our entire defence plan. It was here that we hoped to learn how to make the syrinx work for us.' He turned back to glance at Merlin and Teal. 'And where we failed – or *continue* to fail, I should say. But we had no intention of giving up, not while there was a chance.'

Teal and Merlin were led down into the suspended structure, into a windowless warren of corridors and laboratories. They went down level after level, past sealed doors and observation galleries. There was air and power and light, and clearly enough room for thousands of workers. But although the place was clean and well-maintained, hardly anyone now seemed to be present. It was only when they got very deep that signs of activity began to appear. Here the side-rooms and offices showed evidence of recent use, and now and then uniformed staff members passed them, carrying notes and equipment. But Merlin detected no sign of haste or excitement in any of the personnel.

The lowest chamber of the structure was a curious circular room. Around its perimeter were numerous desks and consoles, with seated staff at least giving the impression of being involved in some important business. They were all facing the middle of the room, whose floor was a single circular sheet of glass, stretched across the abyss of the underlying lava flow. The orange glow of that molten river underlit the faces of the staff, as if reminding them of the perilous location of their workplace. The glass floor only caught Merlin's eye for an instant, though. Of vastly more interest to him was the syrinx, suspended nose-down in a delicate cradle over the middle of the glass. It was too far from the floor to be reached, even if someone had trusted the doubtful integrity of that glass panel. Merlin was just wondering how anyone got close to the syrinx when a flimsy connecting platform was swung out across the glass, allowing a woman to step over the abyss. Tiptoeing lightly, she adjusted something on the syrinx, moving some sort of transducer from one chalked spot to another, before folding the platform away and returning to her console.

All was quiet, with only the faintest whisper of communications from one member of staff to another.

'In the event of an imminent malfunction,' Baskin said, 'the syrinx may be dropped through the pre-weakened glass, into the lava sea. That may or may not destroy it, of course. We don't know. But it would at least allow the workers some chance of fleeing the facility, which would not be the case if we used nuclear charges.'

'I'm glad you've got their welfare at heart,' Merlin said.

'Don't think too kindly of us,' Baskin smiled back. 'This is war. If we thought there was a chance of the facility itself being overrun, then more than just the syrinx would need to be destroyed. Also the equipment, the records, the collective expertise of the workers…'

'You'd drop the entire structure,' Teal said, nodding her

horrified understanding. 'The reason it's fixed the way it is, on those three legs. You'd press a button and drop all these people into that fire.'

'They understand the risks,' Baskin said. 'And they're paid well. Extremely well, I should say. Besides, it's a very good incentive to hasten the work of understanding.'

Merlin felt no kinship with these warring peoples, and little more than contempt for what they had done to themselves across all these centuries. But compared to the Waymakers, Merlin, Teal and Baskin may as well have been children of the same fallen tribe, playing in the same vast and imponderable ruins, not one of them wiser than the others.

'I'll need persuasion that it's real,' he said.

'I never expected you to take my word for it,' Baskin said. 'You may make whatever use of the equipment here you need, within limits, and you may question my staff freely.'

'Easier if you just let me take it for a test ride.'

'Yes, it would – for you.' Baskin reached out and settled a hand on Merlin's shoulder, as if they were two old comrades. 'Shall we agree – a day to complete your inspection?'

'If that's all you'll allow.'

'I've nothing to hide, Merlin. Do you imagine I'd ever expect to dupe a man like you with a fake? Go ahead and make your enquiries – my staff have already been told to offer you complete cooperation.' Baskin touched a hand to the side of his mouth, as if whispering a secret. 'Truth to tell, it will suit many of them if you take the syrinx. Then they won't feel obliged to keep working in this place.'

They were given a room in the facility, while Merlin made his studies of the syrinx. The staff were as helpful as Baskin had promised, and Merlin soon had all the equipment and records he could have hoped for. Short of connecting the syrinx to *Tyrant*'s own diagnostic systems, he was able to run almost every test he could imagine, and the results and records quickly pointed to the same conclusion. The syrinx was the genuine article.

But Merlin did not need a whole day to arrive at that conclusion.

While Baskin kept Teal occupied with endless discussions in Main, learning all that he could from this living speaker, Merlin used the console to dig into Havergal's history, and specifically the background and career of Baskin's long-dead ancestor, King Curtal. He barely needed to access the private records; what was in the public domain was clear enough. Curtal had come to power within a decade of the *Shrike*'s visit to this system.

Merlin waited until they were alone in the evening, just before they were due to dine with Prince Baskin.

'You've been busy all day,' Teal said. 'I take it you've reached a verdict by now?'

'The syrinx? Oh, that was no trouble at all. It's real, just as Baskin promised. But I used my time profitably, Teal. I found out something else as well – and I think you'll find it interesting. You were right about that portrait, you see.'

'I know you enjoy these games, Merlin. But if you want to get to the point ...'

'The man who became King Curtal began life called Tierce.' He watched her face for the flicker of a reaction that he knew she would not be able to conceal. The recognition of a name, across years or centuries, depending on the reckoning.

Merlin cleared his throat before continuing.

'Tierce was a high-ranking officer in the Havergal military command – assigned to the liaison group which dealt with the *Shrike*. He'd have had close contact with your crew during the whole time you were in-system.'

Her mouth moved a little before she found the words. 'Tell me what happened to Tierce.'

'Nothing bad. But what you might not have known about Tierce was that he was also minor royalty. He probably played it down, trying to get ahead in his career on his own merits. And that was how things would have worked out, if it wasn't for one of those craters. A Gaffurian long-range strike, unexpected and deadly, taking out the entire core of the royal family. They were all killed, Teal – barely a decade after you left the system. But they had to maintain continuity, then more than ever. The chain of succession led to Tierce, and he became King Curtal. The man you knew ended up as King.'

She looked at him for a long moment, perhaps measuring for herself the reasons Merlin might have had to lie about such a thing, and then finding none that were plausible, beyond tormenting her for the sake of it.

'Can you be sure?'

'The records are open. There was no cover-up about the succession itself. But the fact that Tierce had a daughter...' Merlin found that he had to glance away before continuing. 'That was difficult. The girl was illegitimate, and that was deeply problematic for the Havergal elite. On the other hand, Tierce was proud and protective of his daughter, and wouldn't accept the succession unless Cupis – that's the girl's name – was given all the rights and privileges of nobility. There was a constitutional tussle, as you can imagine. But eventually it was all settled in favour of Cupis and she was granted legitimacy within the family. They're good at that sort of thing, royals.'

'What you're saying is that Cupis was my daughter.'

'For reasons that you can probably imagine, there's no mention that the child was born to a Cohort mother. That would be a scandal beyond words. But of course you could hardly forget that you'd given birth to a girl, could you?'

She answered after a moment's hesitation. 'We had a girl. Her name was Pauraque.'

Merlin nodded. 'A Cohort name – not much good for the daughter of a king. Tierce would have had to accept a new name for the girl, something more suited to local customs. I don't doubt it was hard for him, if the old name was a link to the person he'd never see again, the person he presumably loved and missed. But he accepted the change in the girl's interests. Do you mind – was there a reason you didn't stay with Tierce, or Tierce didn't join you on the *Shrike*?'

'Neither was allowed,' Teal said, with a sudden coldness in her voice. 'What happened was difficult. Tierce and I were never meant to get that close, and if one of us had stayed with the other it would have made the whole affair a lot more public, risking the trade agreements. We were given no choice. They said if I didn't go along with things, the simplest option would be to make Pauraque disappear. So I had to leave my daughter behind on Havergal, and I was told it would be best for me if I forgot she ever existed. And I tried. But when I saw that portrait...'

'I can't imagine what you went through,' Merlin answered. 'But if I can offer anything by way of consolation, it's this. King Curtal was a good ruler – one of the best they had. And Queen Cupis did just as well. She took the throne late in her father's life, when Curtal abdicated due to failing health. And by all accounts she was an honest and fair-minded ruler who did everything she could to broker peace with the enemy. It was only when the military computers overruled her plans...' Merlin managed a kindly smile and produced the data tablet had been keeping by his side. It was of Havergal manufacture, but rugged and intuitive in its functions. He held it to Teal and a woman's face appeared on the screen. 'That's Queen Cupis,' he said. 'She wasn't one of the portraits we saw earlier, or you'd have made the connection for yourself. I can see you in her pretty clearly.'

Teal took the tablet and held it close to her, so that its glow underlit her features. 'Are there more images?' she asked, with a catch in her voice, as if she almost feared the answer.

'Many,' Merlin replied. 'And recordings, video and audio, taken at all stages in her life. I stored quite a few on the tablet – I thought you'd like to see them.'

'Thank you,' she said. 'I suppose.'

'I know this is troubling for you, and I probably shouldn't have dug into Curtal's past. But once I'd started ...'

'And after Cupis?'

'Nearly twelve hundred years of history, Teal – kings and queens and marriages and assassinations, all down the line. Too many portraits for one room. But your genes were in Cupis and if I've read the family tree properly they ought to be in every descendant, generation after generation.' He paused, giving her time to take this all in. 'I'm not exactly sure what this makes you. Havergal royalty, by blood connection? I'm pretty certain they won't have run into this situation before. Equally certain Baskin doesn't have a clue that you're one of his distant historical ancestors. And I suggest we keep it that way, at least for now.'

'Why?'

'Because it's information,' Merlin said. 'And information's always powerful.'

He left her with the tablet. They were past the hour for their appointment with Prince Baskin now, but Merlin would go on alone and make excuses for Teal's lateness.

Besides, he had something else on his mind.

Merlin and the Prince were dining, just the two of them for the moment. Baskin had been making half-hearted small-talk since Merlin's arrival, but it was plain that there was really only one thing on his mind, and he was straining to have an answer.

'My staff say that you were very busy,' he said. 'Making all sorts of use of our facilities. Did you by any chance ...'

Merlin smiled sweetly. 'By any chance ...?'

'Arrive at a conclusion. Concerning the matter at hand.'

Merlin tore into his bread with rude enthusiasm. 'The matter?'

'The syrinx, Merlin. The syrinx. The thing that's kept you occupied all day.'

Merlin feigned sudden and belated understanding, touching a hand to his brow and shaking his head at his own forgetfulness. 'Of course. Forgive me, Prince Baskin. It always was really just a formality, wasn't it? I mean, I never seriously doubted your honesty.'

'I'm glad to hear that.' But there was still an edge in Baskin's voice. 'So ...'

'So?'

'Is it real, or is it not real. That's what you set out to establish, isn't it?'

'Oh, it's real. Very real.' Merlin looked at his host with a dawning understanding. 'Did you actually have doubts of your own, Prince? That had never occurred to me until now, but I suppose it would have made perfect sense. After all, you only ever had the *Shrike*'s word that the thing was real. How could you ever know, without using it?'

'We tried, Merlin. For thirteen hundred years, we tried. But it's settled, then? You'll accept the syrinx in payment? It really isn't much that I'm asking of you, all things considered.'

'If you really think this bag of tricks will make all the difference, then who I am I to stand in your way?'

Baskin beamed. He stood and recharged their glasses from the bottle that was already half-empty.

'You do a great thing for us, Merlin. Your name will echo down the centuries of peace to follow.'

'Let's just hope the Gaffurians hold it in the same high esteem.'

'Oh, they will. After a generation or two under our control, they'll forget there were ever any differences between us. We'll be generous in victory, Merlin. If there are scores to be settled, it will be with the Gaffurian high command, not the innocent masses. We have no quarrel with those people.'

'And the brigands – you'll extend the same magnanimity in their direction?'

'There'll be no need. After you've taken back the Tactician, they'll be a spent force, brushed to the margins.'

Merlin's smile was tight. 'I did a little more reading on them. There was quite a bit in the private and public records, beyond what you showed me on the crossing.'

'We didn't care to overwhelm you with irrelevant details,' Baskin said, returning to his seat. 'But there was never anything we sought to hide from you. I welcome your curiosity: you can't be too well prepared in advance of your operation.'

'The background is complicated, isn't it? Centuries of dissident or breakaway factions, skulking around the edges of your war, shifting from one ideology to another, sometimes loosely aligned with your side, sometimes with the enemy. At times numerous, at other times pushed almost to extinction. I was interested in their leader, Struxer ...'

'There's little to say about him.'

'Oh, I don't know.' Merlin fingered his glass, knowing he had the edge for now. 'He was one of yours, wasn't he? A military defector. A senior tactician, in his own right. Close to your inner circle – almost a favoured son. But instead of offering his services to the other side, he teamed up with the brigands on Mundar. From what I can gather, there are Gaffurian defectors as well. What do they all want, do you think? What persuades those men and women that they're better off working together, than against each other?'

'They stole the Tactician, Merlin – remember that. A military weapon in all but name. Hardly the actions of untainted pacifists.'

Behind Baskin, the doors opened as Teal came to join them. Baskin twisted around in his seat to greet her, nodding in admiration at the satin Havergal evening wear she had donned for the meal. It suited her well, Merlin thought, but what really mattered was the distraction it offered. While Baskin's attention was diverted, Merlin quickly swapped their glasses. He had been careful to drink to the same level as Baskin, so that the subterfuge wasn't obvious.

'I was just telling Prince Baskin the good news,' Merlin said, lifting the swapped glass and taking a careful sip from it. 'I'm satisfied about the authenticity of the syrinx.'

Teal took her place at the table. Baskin leaned across to pour her a glass. 'Merlin said you were feeling a little unwell, so I wasn't counting on you joining us at all.'

'It was just a turn, Prince. I'm feeling much better now.'

'Good... good.' He was looking at her intently, a frown buried in his gaze. 'You know, Teal, if I didn't know you'd just come from space, I'd swear you were...' But he smiled at himself, dismissing whatever thought he had been about to voice. 'Never mind – it was a foolish notion. I trust you'll accept our hospitality, while Merlin discharges his side of the arrangement? I know you travel together, but on this occasion at least Merlin has no need of an interpreter. There'll be no negotiation, simply a demonstration of overwhelming and decisive force. They'll understand what it is we'd like back.'

'Where he goes, I go,' Teal said.

Merlin tensed, his fingers tight on the glass. 'It might not be a bad idea, actually. There'll be a risk – a small one, I grant, but a risk nonetheless. *Tyrant* isn't indestructible, and I'll be restricted in the weapons I can deploy, if the Prince wants his toy back in one piece. I'd really rather handle this one on my own.'

'I accept the risk,' she said. 'And not because I care about the Tactician, or the difference it will make to this system. But I do want to see the Huskers defeated, and for that Merlin needs his syrinx.'

'I'd have been happy to give it to Merlin now, if I thought your remaining on Havergal would offer a guarantee of his return. But the opposite arrangement suits me just as well. As soon as we have the Tactician, we'll release the syrinx.'

'If those are you terms,' Merlin said, with an easy-going shrug.

Baskin smiled slightly. 'You trust me?'

'I trust the capability of my ship to enforce a deal. It amounts to the same thing.'

'A pragmatist. I knew you were the right man for the job, Merlin.'

Merlin lifted his glass. 'To success, in that case.'

Baskin followed suit, and Teal raised her own glass in half-hearted sympathy. 'To success,' the Prince echoed. 'And victory.'

They left the facility the following morning. Merlin took *Tyrant* this time, Teal joining him as they followed *Renouncer* back into space. Once the two craft were clear of Havergal's atmosphere, Prince Baskin issued a request for docking authorisation. Merlin, who had considered his business with the prince concluded for now, viewed the request with a familiar, nagging trepidation.

'He wants to come along for the ride,' he murmured to Teal, while the airlock cycled. 'Force and wisdom, that's exactly what it'll be. Needs to see Struxer's poor brigands getting their noses bloodied up close and personal, rather than hearing about it from halfway across the system.'

Teal looked unimpressed. 'If he wants to risk his neck, who are you to stop him?'

'Oh, nobody at all. It's just that I work best without an audience.'

'You've already got one, Merlin. Start getting used to it.'

He shrugged aside her point. He was distracted to begin with, thinking of the glass he had smuggled out of the dining room, and whether Prince Baskin had been sharp enough to notice the swap. While they were leaving Havergal he had put the glass into *Tyrant*'s full-spectrum analyser, but the preliminary results were not quite what he had been expecting.

'I wasn't kidding about the risks, you know,' Merlin said.

'Nor was I about wanting to see you get the syrinx. And not because I care about you all that much, either.'

He winced. 'Don't feel you need to spare my feelings.'

'I'm just stating my position. You're the means to an end. You're searching for the means to bring about the destruction of the Huskers. The syrinx is necessary for that search, and therefore I'll help you find it. But if there was a way of *not* involving you...'

'And I thought we broke some ice back there, with all that stuff about Tierce and your daughter.'

'It didn't matter then, it doesn't matter now. Not in the slightest.'

Merlin eyed the lock indicator. 'It isn't as clear-cut as I thought, did you know? I swiped a gene sample from his lordship. Now, if your blood had been percolating its way down the family tree the way it ought to have been, then I should have seen a very strong correlation...'

'Wait,' she said, face hardening as she worked through the implications of that statement. 'You took a sample from him. What about me, Merlin? How did you get a look at my genes, without...?'

'I sampled you.'

Teal slapped him. There had been no warning, and she only hit him the once, and for a moment afterwards it might almost have been possible to pretend that nothing had happened, so exactly had they returned to their earlier stances. But Merlin's cheek stung like a vacuum burn. He opened his mouth, tried to think of something that would explain away her anger.

The lock opened. Prince Baskin came aboard *Tyrant*, wearing his armoured spacesuit with the helmet tucked under one arm.

'There'll be no objections, Merlin. My own ship couldn't keep pace with *Tyrant* even if I wished to shadow you, so the simplest option is to join you for the operation.' He raised a gently silencing hand before Merlin – still stung – had a chance to interject. 'I'll be along purely as an observer, someone with local knowledge, if it comes to that. You don't need to lecture me on the dangers. I've seen my share of frontline service, as you doubtless know, having made yourself such an expert on royal affairs.' He nodded. 'Yes, we tracked your search patterns, while you were supposedly verifying the authenticity of the syrinx.'

'I wanted to know everything I could about your contact with the Cohort mission.'

'That and more, I think.' Baskin mouthed a command into

his neck ring, and *Renouncer* detached from the lock. 'None of it concerns me, though, Merlin. If it amused you to sift through our many assassinations and constitutional crises, so be it. All that matters to me is the safe return of the Tactician. And I will insist on being witness to that return. Don't insult me by suggesting that the presence of one more human on this ship will have any bearing on *Tyrant*'s capabilities.'

'It's not a taxi.'

'But it is spacious enough for our present needs, and that is all that matters.' He nodded at Teal. 'Besides, I was enjoying our evening conversations too much to forego the pleasure.'

'All right,' Merlin said, sighing. 'You're along for the ride, Prince. But I make the decisions. And if I feel like pulling out of this arrangement, for any reason, I'll do just that.'

Prince Baskin set his helmet aside and offered his empty palms. 'There'll be no coercion, Merlin – I could hardly force you into doing anything you disliked, could I?'

'So long as we agree on that.' Merlin gestured to the suite of cabins aft of the lock. 'Teal, show him the ropes, will you? I've got some navigation to be getting on with. We'll push to one gee in thirty minutes.'

Merlin turned his back on Teal and the Prince and returned to *Tyrant*'s command deck. He watched the dwindling trace of the *Renouncer*, knowing he could outpace it with ease. There would be a certain attraction in cutting and running right now, hoping that the old syrinx held together long enough for a Waynet transition, and seeing Baskin's face when he realised he would not be returning to Havergal for centuries, if at all.

But while Merlin was capable of many regrettable things, spite was not one of his failings.

His gaze slid to the results from the analyser. He thought of running the sequence again, using the same traces from the wine glass, but the arrival of the Prince rendered that earlier sample of doubtful value. Perhaps it had been contaminated to begin with, by other members of the royal staff. But now that Baskin was aboard, *Tyrant* could obtain a perfect genetic readout almost without trying.

The words of Baskin returned to mind, as if they held some significance Merlin could not yet see for himself: *If it amused you to sift through our many assassinations and constitutional crises, so be it.*

Assassinations.

When Merlin was satisfied that Prince Baskin's bones were up to the strain, he pushed *Tyrant* to two gees. It was uncomfortable for all of them, but bearable provided they kept to the lounge and avoided moving around too much. 'We could go faster,' Merlin said, as if it was no great achievement. 'But we'd be putting out a little more exotic radiation than I'd like, and I'd rather not broadcast our intentions too strongly. Besides, two gees will get us to Mundar in plenty of time, and if you find it uncomfortable we can easily dial down the thrust for a little while.'

'You make light of this capability,' Prince Baskin said, his hand trembling slightly as he lifted a drinking vessel to his lips. 'Yet this ship is thousands of years beyond anything possessed by either side in our system.'

Merlin tried to look sympathetic. 'Maybe if you weren't busy throwing rocks at each other, you could spend a little time on the other niceties of life, such as cooperation and mutual advancement.'

'We will,' Baskin affirmed. 'I'll bend my life to it. I'm not a zealot for war. If I felt that there was a chance of a negotiated ceasefire, under terms amicable to both sides, I'd have seized it years ago. But our ideological differences are too great, our mutual grievances too ingrained. Sometimes I even think to myself that it wouldn't matter *who* wins, just as long as one side prevails over the other. There are reasonable men and women in Gaffurius, it's just...' But he trailed off, as if even he viewed this line of argument as treasonable.

'If you thought that way,' Teal said, 'the simplest thing would be to let the enemy win. Give them the Iron Tactician, if you think it will make that much difference.'

'After all our advances…? No. It's too late for that sort of idealism. Besides, we aren't dealing with Gaffurius. It's the brigands who are holding us to ransom.'

'Face it,' Merlin said. 'For all this talk of peace, of victory – you'd miss the war.'

'I wouldn't.'

'I'm not so sure. You used to play at battle, didn't you? Toy soldiers and tabletop military campaigns, you said. It's been in your blood from the moment you took your first breath. You were the boy who dreamed of war.'

'I changed,' Baskin said. 'Saw through those old distractions. I spoke of Lurga, didn't I – the last and greatest of our surface cities? Before the abandonment my home was Lurga's imperial palace, a building that was itself as grand as some cities. I often walk it in my dreams, Merlin. But that's where it belongs now: back in my childhood, along with all those toy soldiers.'

'Lurga must have been something to see,' Merlin said.

'Oh, it was. We built and rebuilt. They couldn't bear it, of course, the enemy. That's why Lurga was always the focus of their attacks, right until the end.'

'There was a bad one once, wasn't there?' Merlin asked.

'Too many to mention.'

'I mean, a particularly bad one – a direct strike against the palace itself. It's in your public history – I noticed it while I was going through your open records, on Havergal. You'd have been six or seven at the time, so you'd easily remember it. An assassination attempt, plainly. The Gaffurians were trying to bite the head off the Havergal ruling elite.'

'It was bad, yes. I was injured, quite seriously, by the collapse of part of the palace. Trapped alone and in the dark for days, until rescue squads broke through. I… recovered, obviously. But it's a painful episode and not one I care to dwell on. Good people died around me, Merlin. No child should have to see that.'

'I couldn't agree more.'

'Perhaps it was the breaking of me, in the end,' Baskin said. 'Until then I'd only known war as a series of distant triumphs. Glorious victories and downplayed defeats. After the attack, I knew what blood looked like up close. I healed well enough, but only after months of recuperation. And when I returned to my studies, and some engagement with public life, I found that I'd begun to lose my taste for war. I look back on that little boy that I once was, so single-mindedly consumed by war and strategy, and almost wonder if I'm the same person.' He set aside his drinking vessel, rubbing at the sore muscles in his arm. 'You'll forgive me, both of you. I feel in need of rest. Our ships can only sustain this sort of acceleration for a few tens of minutes, not hour after hour.'

'It's hard on us all,' Merlin said, feeling a glimmer of empathy for his unwanted guest. 'And you're right about one thing, Prince. I want an end to the war with the Huskers. But not at any cost.'

When they were alone Teal said: 'You've got some explaining to do. If it wasn't for Baskin I'd have forced it out of you with torture by now.'

'I'm glad you didn't. All that screaming would have made our guest distinctly uncomfortable. And have you ever tried getting blood out of upholstery?' Merlin flashed a smile. But Teal's hard mask of an expression told him she was in no mood for banter.

'Why were you so interested in his genetic profile?'

There were sealed doors between the lounge and the quarters assigned to the Prince, but the ship was silent under normal operation and Merlin found himself glancing around and lowering his voice before answering.

'I just wanted peace of mind, Teal. I just thought that if I could find a genetic match between you and Prince Baskin, it would settle things for good, allow you to put your mind to rest about Cupis…'

'Put *my* mind to rest.'

'I know I shouldn't have sampled you without your permission. It was just some hair left on your pillow, with a skin flakes…' Merlin silenced himself. 'Now that we're aboard, the ship can run a profile just by sequencing the cells it picks up through the normal air circulation filters.'

Teal still had her arm out, her look defiant. But slowly she pulled back the arm and slid her sleeve back down. 'Run your damned tests. You've started this, you may as well finish it.'

'Are you sure, Teal? It may not get us any nearer an answer of what happened to your bloodline.'

'I said finish it,' Teal answered.

Tyrant slipped across the system, into the contested space between the two stars. Battle continued to rage across a dozen worlds and countless more moons, minor planets and asteroids. Fleets were engaging on a dozen simultaneous fronts, their energy bursts spangling the night sky across light hours of distance. Every radio channel crackled with military traffic, encrypted signals, blatant propaganda, screams of help or mercy from stricken crews.

Tyrant steered clear of the worst of it. But even as they approached Mundar, Merlin picked out more activity than he had hoped for. Gaffurian patrol groups were swinging suspiciously close to the brigands' asteroid, as if something had begun to attract their interest. So far they were keeping clear of the predicted defence perimeter, but their presence put Merlin on edge. It didn't help that the Gaffurian incursions were drawing a counter-response from Havergal squadrons. The nearest battlefronts were still light-minutes away, but the last thing Merlin needed was a new combat zone opening up right where he had business of his own.

'I was hoping for a clear theatre of action,' he told Baskin.

'Something nice and quiet, where I could do my business without a lot of messy distractions.'

'Gaffurian security may have picked up rumours about the Tactician by this point,' Baskin said.

'And that wasn't worth sharing with me before now?'

'I said rumours, Merlin – not hard intelligence. Or they may just be taking a renewed interest in the brigands. They're as much a thorn in the enemy's side as they are in ours.'

'I like them more and more.'

They were a day out when Merlin risked a quick snoop with *Tyrant's* long-range sensors. Baskin and Teal were on the command deck as the scans refreshed and updated, overlaid with the intelligence schematics Merlin had already examined on the *Renouncer.* Mundar was a fuzzy rock traced through with the equally ghostly fault-lines of shafts, corridors, internal pressure vaults and weapons emplacements.

'That was a risky thing to do' Baskin said, while Teal nodded her agreement.

'If they picked up anything,' Merlin said, 'it would have been momentary and on a spread of frequencies and particle bands they wouldn't normally expect. They'll put it down to sensor malfunctions and move on.'

'I wish I had your confidence.'

Merlin stretched out his hands and cracked his knuckles, as if he were preparing to climb a wall. 'Let's think like Struxer. He's got his claws on something precious, a one-off machine, so chances are he won't put the Tactician anywhere vulnerable, especially with these patrol groups sniffing around.'

'How does that help us?'

'Because it narrows down his options. That deep vault there – do you think it would suit?'

'Perhaps. The main thing is to declare our intentions; to give Struxer an unambiguous idea of your capabilities.' Baskin danced his own finger across the display. 'You'll open with a decisive but pin-point attack. Enough to shake them up, and let them know we absolutely mean business. At what distance can you launch a strike?'

'We'll be in optimum charm-torp range in about six hours. I can lock in the targeting solutions now, if you like. But we'll have a sharper view of Mundar the nearer we get.'

'Would they be able to see us that soon?' Teal asked.

Merlin was irritated by the question, but only because it had been the next thing on his mind.

'From what we understand of your ship's sensor footprint, they'll be able to pick you out inside a volume of radius one and a half light seconds. That's an estimate, though. Their weapons will be kinetic launchers, pulse beams, drone missiles. Can you deal with that sort of thing?'

'Provided I'm not having a bad day.'

Baskin extended his own finger at the scans, wavering under the effort. 'These cratered emplacements are most likely the sites of their kinetic batteries. I suggest a surgical strike against all of them, including the ones around the other side of Mundar. Can you do it?'

'Twelve charm-torps should take care of them. Which is handy, because that's all I've got left. We'll still have the gamma-cannons and the nova-mine launchers, if things get sticky.'

'If I know Struxer, they will.' Something twitched in Baskin's cheek, some nervous, betraying tic. 'But the deaths will be all on his side, not ours. If that's the cost of enforcing peace, so be it.'

Merlin eyed him carefully. 'I've never been very good with that sort of calculus.'

'None of us like it,' Baskin said.

Teal went off to catch some sleep until they approached the attack threshold. Merlin grabbed a few hours as well, but his rest was fitful and he soon found himself returning to the command deck, watching as the scans slowly sharpened and their view of Mundar grew more precise. *Tyrant* was using passive sensors now, but these were already improving on the earlier active snapshot. Merlin was understandably on edge, though. They were backing toward the asteroid, and if there was ever a chance of their exhaust emissions being picked up, now was the time. Merlin had done what he could, trading deceleration efficiency for a constantly altering thrust angle that ought to provide maximum cover, but nothing was guaranteed.

'I thought I'd find you here,' Baskin said, pinching at the corners of his eyes as he entered the room. 'You've barely slept since we left Havergal, have you?'

'You don't look much more refreshed, Prince.'

'I know – I saw myself in the mirror just now. Sometimes when I look at my own portrait, I barely recognise myself. I think I can be excused a little anxiety, though. So much depends on the next few hours, Merlin. I think these may be the most critical hours of my entire career. My entire life, even.'

Merlin waited until the Prince had taken his seat, folding his bones with care. 'You mentioned Struxer back there.'

'Did I?'

'The intelligence briefings told me very little, Prince – even the confidential files I lifted from your sealed archives on Havergal. But you spoke as if you knew the man.'

'Struxer was one of us. That was never any sort of secret.'

'A senior tactician, that's what I was told. That sounds like quite a high-up role to me. Struxer wasn't just some anonymous military minion, was he?'

After a moment Baskin said: 'He was known to me. As of course were all the high-ranking strategists.'

'Was Struxer involved in the Tactician?'

If Baskin meant to hide his hesitation, he did a poor job of it. 'To a degree. The Tactician required a large staff, not just to coordinate the feeding-in of intelligence data, but to analyse and act on the results. The battle computers I mentioned...'

'But Struxer was close to it all, wasn't he?' Merlin was guessing now, relying on hard-won intuition, but Baskin's reactions were all he needed to know he was on the right track. 'He worked closely with the computer.'

'His defection was… regrettable.'

'If you can call it a defection. That would depend on what those brigands actually want, wouldn't it? And no one's been terribly clear on that with me.'

Baskin's face was strained. 'They're against peace. Is there anything more you need to know?'

Merlin smiled, content with that line of questioning for now. 'Prince, might I ask you something else? You know I took an interest in your constitutional history when we were on Havergal. Assassinations are commonplace, aren't they? There was that time when almost the entire ruling house of Havergal was wiped out in one strike…'

'That was twelve or thirteen centuries ago.'

'But only a little after the visitation of the Shrike. That was why it caught my eye.'

'No other reason?'

'Should there be?'

'Don't play games with me, Merlin – you'll always lose. I was the boy who dreamed of war, remember.'

The door behind them opened. It was Teal, awake sooner than Merlin had expected. Her face had a freshly scrubbed look, her hair wetted down.

'Are we close?'

'About thirty minutes out,' Merlin said. 'Buckle in, Teal – it could get interesting from any point onwards, especially if their sensors are a little better than the Prince believes.'

Teal slipped into the vacant seat. Befitting her Cohort training, she had adapted well to the two gees, moving around *Tyrant* with a confident, sinewy ease.

'Have you run that genetic scan again?' she asked.

'I have,' Merlin said. 'And I came up with the same result, only at a higher confidence level. Do you want to tell him, or should I?'

'Tell me what?' Baskin asked.

'There's a glitch in your family tree,' Merlin said, then nodded at Teal for her to continue.

'I've already been to your world,' she said, delivering the words with a defiant and brazen confidence. 'I was on the diplomatic party, aboard the swallowship *Shrike*. I was with them when they sold you the syrinx.' Before he had a chance to voice his disbelief, she said: 'A little later, our ship ran into trouble in a nearby system. The Huskers took us, wrecked the ship, but left just enough of us alive to suffer. We went into frostwatch, those of us who remained. And one by one we died, when the frostwatch failed. I was the last living survivor. Then Merlin found me, and we returned to your system. You know this to be possible, Prince. You know of frostwatch, of near-light travel, of time-compression.'

'I suppose...' he said.

'But there's more to it than that,' Teal went on. 'My daughter stayed on Havergal. She became Cupis, Queen Cupis, after Tierce was promoted to the throne. You said it yourself, Prince: there was something in my face you thought you recognised. It's your own lineage, your own family tree.'

'Except it isn't, quite,' Merlin said. 'You see, you're not related, and you should be. I ran a genetic cross-match between the two of you on Havergal, and another since you've been on *Tyrant*. Both say there's no correlation, which is odd given the family tree. But I think there's a fairly simple explanation.'

Baskin glanced from Merlin to Teal and back to Merlin, his eyes wide, doubting and slightly fearful. 'Which would be?'

'You're not Prince Baskin,' Merlin said. 'You just think you are.'

'Don't be absurd. My entire life has been lived in the public eye, subject to the harshest scrutiny.'

Merlin did his best not to sound too callous, nor give the impression that he took any pleasure in disclosing what he now knew to be the truth. 'There's no doubt, I'm afraid. If you were really of royal blood, I'd know it. The only question is where along your family tree the birth line was broken, and why. And I think I know the answer to that, as well ...'

The console chimed. Merlin turned to it with irritation, but a glance told him that the ship had every reason to demand his attention. A signal was beaming out at them, straight from Mundar.

'That isn't possible,' Baskin said. 'We're still three light seconds out – much too far for their sensors.'

Teal said: 'Perhaps you should see what it says.'

The transmission used local protocols, but it only took an instant for *Tyrant* to unscramble the packets and resolve them into a video signal. A man's head appeared above the console, backdropped by a roughly hewn wall of pale rock. Merlin recognised the face as belonging to Struxer, but only because he had paid close attention to the intelligence briefings. Otherwise it would have been easy to miss the similarities. This Struxer was thinner of face, somehow more delicate of bone structure, older and wearier looking, than the cold-eyed defector Merlin had been expecting.

He started speaking in a high steady voice, babbling out a string of words in the Havergal tongue. *Tyrant* was listening in, but it would be a little while before it could offer a reliable translation.

Merlin turned to Teal.

'What's he saying?'

'I'm just as capable of telling you,' Baskin said.

Merlin nodded. 'But I'd sooner hear it from Teal.'

'He's got a fix on you,' she said, frowning slightly as she caught up with the stream of words. 'Says he's had a lock since the moment you were silly enough to turn those scanning systems onto Mundar. Says you must have thought they were idiots, to miss something that obvious. Also that we're not as stealthy as we think we are, judging by the ease with which he's tracking our engine signature.'

'You fool,' Baskin hissed. 'I told you it was a risk.'

'He says he knows what our intentions are,' Teal went on. 'But no matter how much force you throw at them they're not going to relinquish the Iron Tactician. He says to turn back now, and avoid unnecessary violence.'

Merlin gritted teeth. 'Ship, get ready to send a return transmission using the same channel and protocols. Teal, you're doing the talking. Tell Struxer I've no axe to grind with him or his brigands, and if we can do this without bloodshed no one'll be happier than me. Also that I can take apart that asteroid as easily as if it's a piece of rotten fruit.'

Baskin gave a thin smile, evidently liking Merlin's tone.

'Belligerent enough for you, was it?' Merlin asked, while Teal leaned in and translated Merlin's reply.

'Threats and force are what they understand,' Baskin said.

It took three seconds for Teal's statement to reach Mundar, and another three for Struxer's response to find its way back to *Tyrant*. They listened to what he had to say, Merlin needing no translator to tell him that Struxer's answer was a great deal more strident than before.

'You can forget about them handing it over without a struggle,' Teal said. 'And he says that we'd be very wise not to put Mundar's armaments to the test, now that the Iron Tactician's coordinating its own defence plans. They've got every weapon on that asteroid hooked directly into the Tactician, and they're prepared to let it protect itself.'

'They'd still be outgunned,' Merlin said. But even he couldn't quite disguise the profound unease he was beginning to feel.

'It's a bluff,' Baskin said. 'The Tactician has no concept of its own self-preservation.'

'Can you be sure?' Teal asked.

'Tell Struxer this,' Merlin said. 'Surrender the Iron Tactician and I won't lay a finger on that asteroid. All they have to do is bring it to the surface – my proctors can take care of the rest.'

Teal relayed the statement. Struxer barked back his answer,

which was monosyllabic enough to require no translation.

'He says if we want it, we should try taking it,' Teal said.

Merlin nodded – he had been expecting as much, but it had seemed worth his while to make one last concession at a negotiated settlement. 'Ship, give me manual fire control on the torp racks. We're a little further out than I'd like, but it'll give me time to issue a warning. I'm taking out those kinetic batteries.'

'You have control, Merlin,' *Tyrant* said.

Baskin asked: 'Are you sure it isn't too soon?'

Merlin gave his reply by means of issuing the firing command. *Tyrant* pushed out its ventral weapons racks and the charm-torps sped away with barely a twitch of recoil. Only a pattern of moving nodes on the targeting display gave any real hint that the weapons had been deployed.

'Torps armed and running,' *Tyrant* said.

'Teal, tell them they have a strike on its way. They've got a few minutes to move their people deeper into the asteroid, if they aren't already there. My intention is to disable their defences, not to take lives. Make sure Struxer understands that.'

Teal was in the middle of delivering her message when *Tyrant* jolted violently and without warning. It was a sideways impulse, harsh enough to bruise bones, and for a moment Merlin could only stare at the displays, as shocked as he had been when Teal had slapped him across the face.

Then there was another jolt, in the opposite direction, and he understood.

'Evasive response in progress,' *Tyrant* said. 'Normal safety thresholds suspended. Manual override available, but not recommended.'

'What?' Baskin grimaced.

'We're being shot at,' Merlin said.

Tyrant was taking sharp evasive manoeuvres, corkscrewing hard even as it was still engaged in a breakneck deceleration.

'Impossible. We're still too far out.'

'There's nothing coming at us from Mundar. It's something

else. Some perimeter defence screen we didn't even know about.' He directed a reproachful look at Baskin. 'I mean, that *you* didn't know about.'

'Single-use kinetics, perhaps,' Baskin said. 'Free-floating sentries.'

'I should be seeing the activation pulses. Electromagnetic and optical burst signatures. I'm not. All I'm seeing are the slugs, just before they hit us.'

They were, as far as *Tyrant* could tell, simply inert slugs of dense matter, lacking guidance or warheads. They were falling into detection range just in time to compute and execute an evasion, but the margins were awfully fine.

'There are such things as dark kinetics,' Baskin said. 'They're a prototype weapon system: mirrored and cloaked to conceal the launch pulse. But Struxer's brigands have nothing in their arsenal like that. Even if they had a local manufacturing capability, they wouldn't have the skills to make their own versions ...'

'Would the Tactician know about those weapons?' Teal asked.

'In its catalogue of military assets... yes. But there's a world of difference between knowing of something and being able to direct the duplication and manufacture of that technology.'

'Tell that to your toy,' Merlin murmured. He hoped it was his imagination, but the violent counter-manoeuvres seemed to be coming more rapidly, as if *Tyrant* was having an increasingly difficult time steering between the projectiles. 'Ship, recall six of the charm-torps. Bring them back as quickly as you can.'

'What good will that do?' Baskin snapped. 'You should be hitting them with everything you've got, not pulling your punch at the last minute.'

'We need the torps to give us an escort screen,' Merlin said. 'The other six can still deal with all the batteries on the visible face.'

It had been rash to commit all twelve in one go, he now knew, born of an arrogant assumption as to his own capabilities.

But he had realised his mistake in time.

'Struxer again,' Teal said. 'He says it's only going to get worse, and we should call off the other missiles and give up on our attack. Says if he sees a clear indication of our exhaust, he'll stand down the defence screen.'

'Carry on,' Baskin said.

'Charm-torps on return profile,' *Tyrant* said. 'Shall I deploy racks for recovery?'

'No. Group the torps in a protective cordon around us, close enough that you can interdict any slugs that you can't steer us past. And put in a reminder to me to upgrade our attack countermeasures.'

'Complying. The remaining six torps are now being reassigned to the six visible targets. Impact in... twenty seconds.'

'Struxer,' Merlin said, not feeling that his words needed any translation. 'Get your people out of those batteries!'

A sudden blue brightness pushed through *Tyrant*'s windows, just before they shuttered tight in response.

'Slug interdicted,' the ship said calmly. 'One torp depleted from defence cordon. Five remaining.'

'Spare me the countdown,' Merlin said. 'Just get us through this mess and out the other side.'

The six remaining charm-torps of the attack formation closed in on Mundar in the same instant, clawing like a six-taloned fist, gouging six star-hot wounds into the asteroid's crust, six swelling spheres of heat and destruction that grew and dimmed until they merged at their boundaries. Merlin, studying the readouts, could only swallow in horror and awe, reminded again of the potency of even modest Cohort weaponry. Megatonnes of rock and dust were boiling off the asteroid even as he watched, like a skull bleeding out from six eye-sockets.

Three of the cordon torps were lost before *Tyrant* began to break free into relatively safe space, but by then Merlin's luck was stretching perilously thin. The torps could interdict the slugs for almost any range of approach vectors, but not always safely. If the impact happened close enough to *Tyrant*, that was not much better than a direct hit.

They were through, then, but not without cost. The hull had taken a battering from two of the nearer detonations, and while none of the damage would ordinarily been of concern, Merlin had been counting on having a ship in optimum condition. Limping away to effect repairs was scarcely an option now.

The consolation, if he needed one, was that Mundar had taken a much worse battering.

'Is Struxer still sending?' Merlin asked.

'He's trying,' Teal said.

Struxer's face appeared, but speckled by interference. He looked strained, glancing either side of him as he made his statement. Teal listened carefully.

'He says they've still got weapons, if we dare to come any nearer. His position hasn't changed.'

'Mine has,' Merlin said. 'Ship, send in the remaining torps, dialled to maximum yield. Strike at the existing impact sites: see if we can't open some fracture plains, or punch our way deep inside.' Then he enlarged the asteroid's schematic and began tapping his finger against some of the secondary installations on the surface – what the intelligence dossiers said were weapons, sensor pods, airlocks. 'Ready nova-mines for dispersal. Spread pattern three. We'll pick off any moving targets with the gamma-cannon.'

Teal said: 'If you hit Struxer's antenna you'll take away our means of communicating.'

'I'm past the point of negotiation, Teal. My ship's wounded and I take that personally. If you want to send a last message to Struxer, tell him he had his chance to play nicely.'

Baskin leaned forward in his seat restraints. 'Don't do anything too rash, Merlin. We came to force his hand, not to annihilate the entire asteroid.'

'Your primary consideration was stopping the Tactician falling into the wrong hands. I'm about to guarantee that never happens.'

'I want it intact.'

'It was never going to work, Prince. There was never going to be any magic peace, just because you had your battle computer back.' A sudden indignation passed through him. 'I know wars. I know how they play out. Squeeze the enemy hard and they just find new ways to fight back. It'll go on and on and you'll never be any nearer victory.'

'We were winning.'

'One tide was going out. Another was due to come back in. That's all it was.'

The charm-torps were striking. Set to their highest explosive setting, the bursts were twenty times brighter than the first wave. Each fireball scooped out a tenth of the asteroid's volume, lofting unthinkable quantities of rock and dirt and gas into space, a ghastly swelling shroud lit from within by pulses of lightning.

Lines of light cut through that shroud. Kinetics and lasers were striking out from what remained of the asteroid's facing hemisphere, sweeping in arcs as they tried to find *Tyrant*. The ship swerved and stabbed like a dancing snake. The edge of a laser gashed across part of its hull, triggering a shriek of damage alarms. Merlin dispatched the nova-mines, then swung the nose around to bring the gamma-cannon into play. The flashes of the nova-mines began to pepper the shrouded face of Mundar. The kinetics and lasers were continuing, but their coverage was becoming sparser. Merlin sensed that they had endured the worst of the assault. But the approach had enacted a grave toll on *Tyrant*. One more direct hit, even with a low-energy weapon, might be enough to split open the hull.

Tyrant had reduced its speed to only a few kilometres per second relative to the asteroid. Now they were beginning to pick up the billowing front of the debris cloud. *Tyrant* was built to tolerate extremes of pressure, but the hot, gravelly medium was nothing like an atmosphere. Under other circumstances Merlin would have gladly turned around rather than push deeper. But

Tyrant would have to cross the kinetic defence screen to reach empty space, and now he had used up all his charm-torps. If the Tactician had indeed been coordinating Mundar's defences, then Merlin saw only one way to dig himself out of this hole. He could leave nothing intact – even if it meant butchering whoever was left alive in Mundar.

Debris hammered the hull. Merlin curled fingers into sweat-sodden palms.

'Merlin,' Teal said. 'It's Struxer's signal again. Only it's not coming from inside Mundar.'

Merlin understood as soon as he shifted his attention to the navigational display. Struxer's transmission was originating from a small moving object, coming toward them from within the debris field. The gamma-cannon was still aimed straight at Mundar. Merlin shifted the lock onto the object, ready to annihilate it in an instant. Then he waited for *Tyrant*'s sensors to give him their best estimate of the size and form of the approaching object. He was expecting something like a mine or a small autonomous missile, trying to camouflage its approach within the chaos of the debris. But then why was it transmitting in the first place?

He had his answer a moment later. The form was five-nubbed, a fat-limbed starfish. Or a human, wearing a spacesuit, drifting through the debris cloud like a rag doll in a storm.

'Suicidal,' Baskin said.

There was no face now, just a voice. The signal was too poor for anything else. Teal listened and said: 'He's asking for you to slow and stand down your weapons. He says we've reached a clear impasse. You'll never make it out of this area without the Tactician's cooperation, and you'll never find the Tactician without his assistance.'

Merlin had manual fire control on the gamma-cannon. He had settled one hand around the trigger, ready to turn that human starfish into just another crowd of hot atoms.

'I said I was past the point of negotiation.'

'Struxer says dozens have already died in the attack. But

there are thousands more of his people still alive in the deeper layers. He says you won't be able to destroy the Tactician without killing them as well.'

'They picked this fight, not me.'

'Merlin, listen to me. Struxer seems reasonable. There's a reason he's put himself out there in that suit.'

'I blew up his asteroid. That might have something to do with it.'

'He wants to negotiate from a position of weakness, not strength. That's what he says. Every moment where you *don't* destroy him is another moment in which you might start listening.'

'I think we already stated our positions, didn't we?'

'He said you wouldn't be able to take the Tactician. And you can't, that's clear. You can destroy it, but you can't take it. And now he's asking to talk.'

'About what?'

Teal looked at him with pleading eyes. 'Just talk to him, Merlin. That woman you showed me – your mother, waiting by that window. The sons she lost – you and your brother. I saw the kindness in her. Don't tell me you'd have made her proud by killing that man.'

'My mother died on Plenitude. She wasn't in that room. I showed you nothing, just ghosts, just memories stitched together by my brother.'

'Merlin…'

He squeezed the fire control trigger. Instead of discharging, though, the gamma-cannon reported a malfunction. Merlin tried again, then pulled his shaking, sweat-sodden hand from the control. The weapons board was showing multiple failures and system errors, as if the ship had only just been holding itself together until that moment.

'You cold-hearted …' Teal started.

'Your sympathies run that deep,' Merlin said. 'You should have spoken up before we used the torps.'

Baskin levelled a hand on Merlin's wrist, drawing him further from the gamma-cannon trigger. 'Perhaps it was for the best, after all. Only Struxer really knows the fate of the Tactician now. Bring him in, Merlin. What more have we got to lose?'

Struxer removed his helmet, the visor pocked and crazed from his passage through the debris cloud. Merlin recognised the same drawn, weary face that had spoken to them from within Mundar. He made an acknowledgement of Prince Baskin, speaking in the Havergal tongue – Merlin swearing that he picked up the sarcasm and scorn despite the gulf of language.

'He says it was nice of them to send royalty to do their dirty work,' Teal said.

'Tell him he's very lucky not to be a cloud of atoms,' Merlin said.

Teal passed on this remark, listened to the answer, then gave a half smile of her own. 'Struxer says you're very lucky that the Tactician gave you safe passage.'

'That's his idea of safe passage?' Merlin asked.

But he moved to a compartment in the cabin wall and pulled out a tray of coiled black devices, each as small and neat as a stone talisman. He removed one of the translators and pressed it into his ear, then offered one of the other devices to Struxer.

'Tell him it won't bite,' he said. 'My ship's very good with languages, but it needs a solid baseline of data to work with. Those transmissions helped, but the more we talk, the better we'll get.'

Struxer fingered the translator in the battered glove of his spacesuit, curling his lips in distrust. 'Cohort man,' he said, in clear enough Main. 'I speak a little your language. The Prince made us take school. In case Cohort come back.'

'So you'd have a negotiating advantage over the enemy?' Merlin asked.

'It seemed prudent,' Baskin said. 'But most of my staff didn't see it that way. Struxer was one of the exceptions.'

'Be careful who you educate,' Merlin told him. 'They have a tendency to start thinking for themselves. Start doing awkward things like defecting, and holding military computers to ransom.'

Struxer had pushed the earpiece into position. He shifted back to his native tongue, and his translated words buzzed into Merlin's skull. 'Ransom – is that what you were told, Cohort man?'

'My name's Merlin. And yes – that seems to be the game here. Or did you steal the Tactician because you'd run out of games to play on a rainy afternoon?'

'You have no idea what you've been drawn into. What were you promised, to do his dirty work?'

Teal said: 'Merlin doesn't need you. He just wants the Tactician.'

'A thing he neither understands nor needs, and which will never be his.'

'I'd still like it,' Merlin said.

'You're too late,' Struxer said. 'The Tactician has decided its own fate now. You've brought those patrol groups closer, with that crude display of strength. They'll close on Mundar soon enough. But the Tactician will be long gone by then.'

'Gone?' Baskin asked.

'It has accepted that it must end itself. Mundar's remaining defences are now being turned inward, against the asteroid itself. It would rather destroy itself than become of further use to Havergal, or indeed Gaffurius.'

'Ship,' Merlin said. 'Tell me this isn't true.'

'I would like to,' *Tyrant* said. 'But it seems to be the case. I am recording an increasing rate of kinetic bombardments against Mundar's surface. Our own position is not without hazard, given my damaged condition.'

Merlin moved to the nearest console, confirming for himself what the ship already knew. The opposed fleets were altering course, pincering in around Mundar. Anti-ship weapons were already sparking between the two groups of ships, drawing both into closer and closer engagement.

'The Tactician will play the patrol groups off each other, drawing them into an exchange of fire,' Struxer said, with an icy sort of calm. 'Then it will parry some of that fire against Mundar, completing the work you have begun.'

'It's a machine,' Baskin said. 'It can't decide to end itself.'

'Oh, come now,' Struxer said, regarding Baskin with a shrewd, skeptical scrutiny. 'We're beyond those sorts of secrets, aren't we? Or are you going to plead genuine ignorance?'

'Whatever you think he knows,' Merlin said, 'I've a feeling he doesn't.'

Struxer shifted his attention onto Merlin. 'Then you know?'

'I've an inkling or two. No more than that.'

'About what?' Teal asked.

Merlin raised his voice. 'Ship, start computing an escape route for us. If the kinetics are being directed at Mundar, then the defence screen ought to be a little easier to get through, provided we're quick.'

'You're running?' Baskin asked. 'With the prize so near?'

'In case you missed it,' Merlin said, 'the prize just got a death-wish. I'm cutting my losses before they cut me. Buckle in, all of you.'

'What about your syrinx?' Teal demanded.

'I'll find me another. It's a big old galaxy – bound to be a few more knocking around. Ship, are you ready with that solution?'

'I am compromised, Merlin. I have hull damage, weapons impairment and a grievous loss of thruster authority. There can be no guarantee of reaching clear space, especially with the build-up of hostile assets.'

'I'll take that chance, thanks. Struxer: you're free to step back out of the airlock any time you like. Or did you think all your problems were over just because I didn't shoot you with the gamma-cannon?'

Tyrant began to move. Merlin steadied a hand against a wall, ready to tense if the gee-loads climbed sharply.

'I think our problems are far from over,' Struxer answered him levelly. 'But I do not wish to die just yet. Equally, I would ask one thing.'

'You're not exactly in a position to be asking for anything.'

'You had a communications channel open to me. Give me access to that same channel and allow me to make my peace with the Tactician, before it's too late. A farewell, if you wish. I can't talk it out of this course of action, but at least I can ease its conscience.'

'It has no conscience,' Baskin said, grimacing as the acceleration mounted and *Tyrant* began to swerve its away around obstacles and in-coming fire.

'Oh, it most definitely does,' Struxer said.

Merlin closed his eyes. He was standing at the door to his mother's parlour, watching her watching the window. She had become aware of his silent presence and bent around in her stern black chair, her arms straining with the effort. The golden sun shifted across the changing angles of her face. Her eyes met his for an instant, liquid grey with sadness, the eyes of a woman who had known much and seen the end of everything. She made to speak, but no words came.

Her expression was sufficient, though. Disappointed, expectant, encouraging, a loving mother well used to her sons' failings, and always hopeful that the better aspects of their nature might rise to the surface. Merlin and Gallinule, last sons of Plenitude.

'Damn it all,' Merlin said under his breath. 'Damn it all.'

'What?' Teal asked.

'Turn us around, ship,' he said. 'Turn us around and take us back to Mundar. As deep as we can go.'

They fought their way into the thick broil of the dust cloud, relying on sensors alone, a thousand fists hammering their displeasure against the hull, until at last *Tyrant* found the docking bay. The configuration was similar to the *Renouncer*, easily within the scope of adjustments that *Tyrant* could make, and they were soon clamped on. Baskin was making ready to secure his vacuum suit when Merlin tossed him a dun-coloured outfit.

'Cohort immersion suit. Put it on. You as well, Struxer. And be quick about it.'

'What are these suits?' Baskin asked, fingering the ever-so-ragged, grubby-looking garment.

'You'll find out soon enough.' Merlin nodded at Teal. 'You too, soldier. As soon as *Tyrant* has an electronic lock on the Tactician it can start figuring out the immersion protocols. Won't take too long.'

'Immersion protocols for what?' Baskin asked, with sharpening impatience.

'We're going inside,' Merlin said. 'All of us. There's been enough death today, and most of it's on my hands. I'm not settling for any more.'

It waited beyond the lock, the only large thing in a dimly-lit chamber walled in rock. The air was cold and did not appear to be recirculating. From the low illumination of the chamber, Merlin judged that Mundar was down to its last reserves of emergency power. He shivered in the immersion suit. It was like wearing paper.

'Did I really kill hundreds, Struxer?'

'Remorse, Merlin?'

Something was tight in his throat. 'I never set out of kill. But I know that there's a danger out there beyond almost any human cost. They took my world, my people. Left Teal without a ship or a crew. They'll do the same to every human world in the galaxy, given time. I felt that if I could bring peace to this one system, I'd be doing something. One small act against a vaster darkness.'

'And that excuses any act?'

'I was only trying to do the right thing.'

Struxer gave a sad sniff of a laugh, as if he had lost count of the number of times he had heard such a justification. 'The only right action is not to kill, Merlin. Not on some distant day when it suits you, but here and now, from the next moment on. The Tactician understands that.' Struxer reached up suddenly as if to swat an insect that had settled on the back of his neck. 'What's happening?'

'The immersion suit's connecting into your nervous system,' Merlin said. 'It's fast and painless and there won't be any lasting damage. Do you feel it too, Prince?'

'It might not be painful,' Baskin said. 'But I wouldn't exactly call it pleasant.'

'Trust us,' Merlin said. 'We're good at this sort of thing.'

At last he felt ready to give the Iron Tactician his full attention.

Its spherical form rested on a pedestal in the middle of the chamber, the low light turning its metallic plating to a kind of coppery brown. It was about as large as an escape capsule, with a strange brooding presence about it. There were no eyes or cameras anywhere on it, at least none that Merlin recognised. But he had the skin-crawling sensation of being watched, noticed, contemplated, by an intellect not at all like his own.

He raised his hands.

'I'm Merlin. I know what you are, I think. You should know what I am, as well. I tried to take you, and I tried to hurt your world. I'm sorry for the people I killed. But I stand before you now unarmed. I have no weapons, no armour, and I doubt very much that there's anything I could do to hurt you.'

'You're wasting your words,' Baskin said behind him, rubbing at the back of his neck.

'No,' Struxer said. 'He isn't. The Tactician hears him. It's fully aware of what happens around it.'

Merlin touched the metal integument of the Iron Tactician, feeling the warmth and throb of hidden mechanisms. It hummed and churned in his presence, and gave off soft liquid sounds, like some huge boiler or laundry machine. He stroked his hand across the battered curve of one of the thick armoured plates, over the groove between one plate and the next. The plates had been unbolted or hinged back in places, revealing gold-plated connections, power and chemical sockets, or even rugged banks of dials and controls. Needles twitched and lights flashed, hinting at mysterious processes going on deep within the armour. Here and there a green glow shone through little windows of dark glass.

Tyrant whispered into Merlin's ear, via the translator earpiece. He nodded, mouthed back his answer, then returned his attention to the sphere.

'You sense my ship,' Merlin said. 'It tells me that it understands your support apparatus – that it can map me into your electronic sensorium using this immersion suit. I'd like to step inside, if that's all right?'

No answer was forthcoming – none that Merlin or his ship recognised. But he had made his decision by then, and he felt fully and irrevocably committed to it.. 'Put us through, ship – all of us. We'll take our chances.'

'And if things take a turn for the worse?' *Tyrant* asked.

'Save yourself, however you're able. Scuttle away and find someone else that can make good use of you.'

'It just wouldn't be the same,' *Tyrant* said.

The immersion suits snatched them from the chamber. The dislocation lasted an instant and then Merlin found himself standing next to his companions, in a high-ceilinged room that might well have been an annex of the Palace of Eternal Dusk. But the architectural notes were subtly unfamiliar, the play of light through the windows not that of his home, and the distant line of hills remained resolutely fixed. Marbled floor lay under their feet. White stone walls framed the elegant archwork of the windows.

'I know this place,' Baskin said, looking around. 'I spent a large part of my youth in these rooms. This was the imperial palace in Lurga, as it was before the abandonment.' Even in the sensorium he wore a facsimile of the immersion suit, and he stroked the thin fabric of its sleeve with unconcealed wonder. 'This is a remarkable technology, Merlin. I feel as if I've stepped back into my childhood. But why these rooms – why recreate the palace?'

Only one doorway led out of the room in which they stood. It faced a short corridor, with high windows on one side and doors on the other. Merlin beckoned them forward. 'You should tell him, Struxer. Then I can see how close I've come to figuring it out for myself.'

'Figured what out?' Baskin asked.

'What really happened when they attacked this place,' Merlin said.

They walked into the corridor. Struxer seemed at first loss for how to start. His jaw moved, but no sounds came. Then he glanced down, swallowed, and found the words he needed.

'The attack's a matter of record,' he said. 'The young Prince Baskin was the target, and he was gravely injured. Spent days and days half-buried, in darkness and cold, until the teams found him. Then the prince was nurtured back to strength, and finally allowed back into the world. But that's not really what happened.'

They were walking along the line of windows. The view beyond was vastly more idyllic than any part of the real Havergal. White towers lay amongst woods and lakes, with purple-tinged hills rising in the distance, the sky beyond them an infinite storybook blue.

'I assure you it did,' Baskin said. 'I'd remember otherwise, wouldn't I?'

'Not if they didn't want you to,' Merlin said. He walked on for a few paces. 'There was an assassination strike. But it didn't play out the way you think it did. The real prince was terribly injured – much worse than your memories have it.'

Now an anger was pushing through Baskin's voice. 'What do you mean, the "real prince"?'

'You were substituted,' Struxer said, 'the assassination attempt played down, no mention made of the extent of the real Prince's injuries.'

'My bloodline,' Teal said. 'This is the reason it's broken, isn't it?'

Merlin nodded, but let Struxer continue. 'They rebuilt this palace as best they could. Even then it was never as idealised as this. Most of the east wing was gone. The view through these windows was... less pretty. It was only ever a stopgap, before Lurga had to be abandoned completely.'

They had reached the only open door in the corridor. With the sunlit view behind their backs their shadows pushed across the door's threshold, into the small circular room beyond.

In the middle of the room a small boy knelt surrounded by wooden battlements and toy armies. They ranged away from him in complex, concentric formations – organised into interlocking ranks and files as tricky as any puzzle. The boy was reaching out to move one of the pieces, his hand dithering in the air.

'No,' Baskin whispered. 'This isn't how it is. There isn't a child inside this thing.'

Struxer answered softly. 'After the attack, the real Prince was kept alive by the best doctors on Havergal. It was all done in great secrecy. It had to be. What had become of him, the extent of his injuries, his dependence on machines to keep him alive... all of that would have been far too upsetting for the populace. The war was going badly: public morale was low enough as it was. The only solution, the only way to maintain the illusion, was to bring in another boy. You looked similar enough, so you were brought in to live out his life. One boy swapped for another.'

'That's not what happened.'

'Boys change from year to year, so the ruse was never obvious,' Struxer said. 'But *you* had to believe. So you were raised exactly as the Prince had been raised, in this palace, surrounded by the same things, and told stories of his life just as if it had been your own. Those games of war, the soldiers and campaigns? They were never part of your previous life, but slowly you started to believe an imagined past over the real one – a fiction that you accepted as the truth.'

'You said you grew bored of war,' Teal said. 'That you were a sickly child who turned away from tabletop battles and became fascinated by languages instead. That was the real you breaking through, wasn't it? They could surround you with the instruments of war, try to make you dream of it, but they couldn't turn you into the person you were not – even if most of the time you believed the lie.'

'But not always,' Merlin said, watching as the boy made up his mind and moved one of the pieces. 'Part of you knew, or remembered, I think. You've been fighting against the lie your whole life. But now you don't need to. Now you're free of it.'

Struxer said: 'We didn't suspect at first. Even those of us who worked closely with the Tactician were encouraged to think of it as a machine, an artificial intelligence. The medical staff who were involved in the initial work were either dead or sworn to silence, and the Tactician rarely needed any outside intervention. But there were always rumours. Technicians who had seen too much, glimpsed a little too far into the heart of it. Others – like myself – who started to doubt the accepted version of events, this easy story of a dramatic breakthrough in artificial intelligence. I began to…question. Why had the enemy never made a similar advancement? Why had we never repeated our success? But the thing that finally settled it for me was the Tactician itself. We who were the closest to it… we sensed the changes.'

'Changes?' Baskin asked.

'A growing disenchantment with war. A refusal to offer the simple forecasts our military leaders craved. The Tactian's advice was becoming… quixotic. Unreliable. We adjusted for it, placed less weight on its predictions and simulations. But slowly those of us who were close to it realised that the Tactician was trying to engineer peace, not war.'

'Peace is what we've always striven for,' Baskin said.

'But by one means, total victory,' Struxer said. 'But the Tactician no longer considered such an outcome desirable. The boy who dreamed of war had grown up, Prince. The boy had started to develop the one thing the surgeons never allowed for.'

'A conscience,' Merlin said. 'A sense of regret.'

The boy froze between one move and the next. He turned to face the door, his eyes searching. He was small-boned, wearing a soldier's costume tailored for a child.

'We're here,' Struxer said, raising a hand by way of reassurance. 'Your friends. Merlin spoke to you before, do you remember?'

The boy looked distracted. He moved a piece from one position to another, angrily.

'You should go,' he said. 'I don't want anyone here today. I'm going to make these armies fight each other so badly they'll never want to fight again.'

Merlin was the first to step into the room. He approached the boy carefully, picking his way through the gaps in the regiments. They were toy soldiers, but he could well imagine that each piece had some direct and logical correspondence in the fleets engaging near Mundar, as well as Mundar's own defenses.

'Prince,' he said, stooping down with his hands on his knees. 'You don't have to do this. Not any more. I know you want something other than war. It's just that they keep trying to force you into playing the same games, don't they?'

'When he didn't give the military planners the forecasts they wanted,' Struxer said, 'they tried to coerce him by other means. Electronic persuasion. Direct stimulation of his nervous system.'

'You mean, torture,' Merlin said.

'No,' Baskin said. 'That's not how it was. The Tactician was a machine... just a machine.'

'It was never that,' Merlin replied.

'I knew what needed to be done,' Struxer said. 'It was a long game, of course. But then the Tactician's strength has always been in long games. I defected first, joined the brigands here in

Mundar, and only then did we start putting in place our plans to take the Tactician.'

'Then it was never about holding him to ransom,' Merlin said.

'No,' Struxer said. 'All that would have done is prolong the war. We'd been fighting long enough, Merlin. It was time to embrace the unthinkable: a real and lasting ceasefire. It was going to be a long and difficult process, and it could only be orchestrated from a position of neutrality, out here between the warring factions. It would depend on sympathetic allies on both sides: good men and women prepared to risk their own lives in making tiny, cumulative changes, under the Tactician's secret stewardship. We were ready – eager, even. In small ways we had begun the great work. Admit it, Prince Baskin: the tide of military successes had begun to turn away from you, in recent months. That was our doing. We were winning. And then Merlin arrived.' Struxer set his features in a mask of impassivity. 'Nothing in the Tactician's forecasting predicted *you*, Merlin, or the terrible damage you'd do to our cause.'

'I stopped, didn't I?''

'Only when Mundar had humbled you.'

The room shook, dust dislodging from the stone walls, one or two of the toy soldiers toppling in their ranks. Merlin knew what that was. *Tyrant* was communicating the actual attack suffered by Mundar through to the sensorium. The asteroid's own kinetic weapons were beginning to break through its crust.

'It won't be long now,' he said.

Teal picked her way to Merlin's side and knelt between the battlements and armies, touching a hand to the boy. 'We can help you,' she said. Followed by a glance to Merlin. 'Can't we?'

'Yes,' he said, doubtfully at first, then with growing conviction. 'Yes. Prince Baskin. The real Prince. The boy who dreamed of war, and then stopped dreaming. I believe it, too. There isn't a mind in the universe that isn't capable of change. You want peace in this system? Something real and lasting, a peace built on forgiveness and reconciliation, rather than centuries of simmering enmity? So do I. And I think you can make it happen, but for that you have to live. I have a ship. You saw me coming in – saw my weapons and what they could do. You blooded me good, as well. But I can help you now – help you do what's right. Turn the kinetics away from Mundar, Prince. You don't have to die.'

'I said you should go away,' the boy said.

Teal lifted a hand to his cheek. 'They hurt you,' she said. 'Very badly. But my blood's in you and I won't rest until you've found peace. But not this way. Merlin's right, Prince. There's still time to do good.'

'They don't want good,' the boy answered. 'I gave them good, but they didn't like it.'

'You don't have to concern yourself with them now,' Merlin said, as another disturbance shook the room. 'Turn the weapons from Mundar. Do it, Prince.'

The boy's hand loitered over the wooden battlements. Merlin intuited that these must be the logical representation of Mundar's defense screens. The boy fingered one of the serrated formations, seemingly on the verge of moving it.

'It won't do any good,' he said.

'It will,' Merlin said.

'You've brought them too near,' the boy said, sweeping his other hand across the massed regiments, in all their colours and divisions. 'They didn't know where I was before, but now you've shown them.'

'I made a mistake,' Merlin admitted. 'A bad one, because I wanted something too badly. But I'm here to make amends.'

Now it was Baskin's turn to step closer to the boy. 'We have half a life in common,' he said. 'They stole a life from you, and tried to make me think it was my own. It worked, too. I'm an old man now, and I suppose you're as old as me, deep down. But we have something in common. We've both outgrown war, whether those around us are willing to accept it or not.' He lowered down, upsetting some of the soldiers as he did – the boy glaring for an instant, then seeming to put the matter behind him. 'I want to help you. Be your friend, if such a thing's possible. What Teal said is true: you *do* have her blood. Not mine, now, but it doesn't mean I don't want to help.' He placed his own hand around the boy's wrist, the hand that hovered over the wooden battlements. 'I remember these games,' he said. 'These toys. I played them well. We could play together, couldn't we?' Slowly, with great trepidation, Baskin risked turning one of the battlements around, until its fortifications were facing outward again.

The boy said: 'I wouldn't do it that way.'

'Show me how you would do it,' Baskin said.

The boy took the battlement and shifted its position. Then he took another and placed them in close formation. He looked up at Baskin, seeking both approval and praise. 'See. That's better, isn't it?'

'Much better,' Baskin said.

'You can move that one,' the boy said, indicating one of the other battlements. 'Put it over there, the other way round.'

'Like this?' Baskin asked, with a nervous, obliging smile.

'A little closer. That's good enough.'

Merlin realised that he had been holding his breath while this little exchange was going on. It was too soon to leap to conclusions, but it had been a while since the room last shook. Hardly daring to break the fragile spell, he slipped into a brief subvocal exchange with *Tyrant*. His ship confirmed that the rain of kinetics had ceased.

'Now for the tricky part,' Merlin murmured, as much for himself as his audience. 'Prince, listen to me carefully. Rebuild those defences. Do it as well as you can, because you need to protect yourself. There's hard work to do – very hard work – and you need to be at your strongest.'

'I don't like work,' the boy said.

'None of us do. But if you're bored with this game, I've got a much more interesting one to play. You're going to engineer a peace, and hold it. It's going to be the hardest thing you've ever done but I've no doubt that you'll rise to the challenge.'

Struxer whispered: 'Those fleets aren't exactly ready to set down their arms, Merlin.'

'I'll make them,' he said. 'Just go give the Prince a running start. Then it's over to him.' But he corrected himself. 'Over to all of you, in fact. He'll need all the help he can get, Struxer.' Merlin leaned in closer to the boy, until his mouth was near his ear. 'We're going to lie,' he said, confidingly. 'We're going to lie and they're going to believe us, those fleets. Not forever, but long enough for you to start making peace seem like the easier path. It's a lot to ask, but I know you're up to it.'

The boy's face met Merlin's. 'Lie?'

'You'll understand. *Tyrant*: open a channel out to those ships. The whole binary system, as powerful a signal as you can put out. Hijack every open transmitter you can find. And translate these words, as well as you can.' Then he frowned to himself and turned to Teal. 'No. You should be the one. Better that it comes from a native speaker, than my garbled efforts.'

'What would you like me to say?'

Merlin smiled. He told her. It did not take long.

'This is Teal of the Cohort,' she said, her words gathered within the sensorium, fed through *Tyrant*, pushed out beyond the ruins of Mundar, through the defense screens, out to the waiting fleets, onward to the warring worlds. 'I came here by Waynet, a little while ago. But I was here once before, more than a thousand years ago, and I knew King Curtal before you set him on the throne. I stand now in Mundar, ready to tell you that the time has come to end this war. Not for an hour, or a day, or a few miserable years, but forever. Because what you need now is peace and unity, and you don't have very long to build it. A Husker attack swarm is approaching your binary system. We slipped ahead of them through the Waynet, but they will be here. You have less than a century… perhaps only a handful of decades. Then they'll arrive.' Teal shot a look at Merlin, and he gave her a tiny nod, letting her know that she was doing very well, better than he could ever have managed. 'Ordinarily it would be the end of everything for you. They took my ship, and I'm with a man who lost a whole world to them. But there's a chance for you. In Mundar is a great mind. Call him the Iron Tactician for now, although the day will come when you learn his true name. The Iron Tactician will help you on the road to peace. And when that peace is holding, the Iron Tactician will help you prepare. The Tactician knows of your weapons, of your fusion ships and kinetic batteries. But in a little while he will also know the weapons of the Cohort, and how best to use them. Weapons to shatter worlds – or defend them.' Teal drew breath, and Merlin touched his hand to her shoulder, in what he hoped was a gesture of comradeship and solidarity. 'Hurt the Tactician, and you'll be powerless when the swarm arrives. Protect it – honour it – and you'll have an honest chance. But the Tactician would sooner die than take sides.'

'Good,' Merlin breathed.

'He's my blood,' Teal continued. 'My kin. And I'm staying here to give him all the protection and guidance he needs. You'll treat me well, because I'm the only living witness you'll ever know who can say she saw the Huskers up close. And I'll do what I can to help you.'

Merlin swallowed. He had not been expecting this, not at all. But the force of Teal's conviction left him in no doubt that she had set her mind on this course. He stared at her with a searing admiration, dizzy at her courage and single-mindedness.

'You'll withdraw from the space around Mundar,' Teal said. 'And you'll cease all hostilities. A ship will be given free passage to Havergal, and then on to the Waynet. You won't touch it. And you won't touch Mundar, or attempt to claim the Tactician. There'll be no reminders, no second warnings – we're beyond such things. This is Teal of the Cohort, signing off for now. You'll be hearing more from me soon.'

Merlin shook his head in astonishment. 'You don't have to

do this, Teal. That was… courageous. But you're not responsible for the mess they've made of this place.'

'I'm not,' she said. 'But then again we had our chance when we traded with them, and instead of helping them to peace we took one side and conducted our business. I don't feel guilty for what happened all those years ago. But I'm ready to make a change.'

'She does have an excellent command of our language,' Baskin said.

'And she's persuasive,' Struxer said. 'Very persuasive.'

Merlin made sure they were no longer transmitting. 'You all know it's a lie. There's no attack swarm heading this way – not how Teal said it was. But there *could* be, and for a few decades there'd be no way of saying otherwise, not with the sensors you have now. Here's what matters, though. You've been lucky so far, but somewhere out there you can be sure there is a Husker swarm that'll eventually find its way to these worlds. A hundred years, a thousand… Who knows? But it will happen, just as it did to Plenitude. The only difference is, you'll be readier than we ever were.' Then he turned to direct his attention to the boy. 'You'll have the hardest time of all, Prince. But you have friends now. And you have my confidence. I know you can force this peace.'

For all the toys and battlements, some spark of real comprehension glimmered in the boy's eyes. 'But when they find out she lied…'

'It'll take a while,' Merlin said. 'And by then you'll just have to make sure they've got used to the idea of peace. It's not such a bad thing. But then again, you don't need me to tell you that.'

'No,' the boy reflected.

Merlin nodded, hoping the boy – what remained of the boy – felt something of the confidence and reassurance he was sending out. 'I have to go soon. There's something I need on Havergal, and I'd rather not wait too long to get my hands on it.'

'Whatever authority I still have,' Baskin said, 'I'll do all that I can to assist.'

'Thank you.' Then Merlin turned back to the Prince. 'I hope you won't be alone again. I'll leave the immersion suits behind, and a few spares. But even when Teal and Struxer and Baskin can't be with you, you don't have to be without companionship.' He dipped his head at the ranged formations. 'There are two other boys who used to enjoy games like this, but like you their hearts were always elsewhere. They could come here, if you like. I think you'd get on well.'

Doubt flickered across Teal's brow. He nodded at her, begging her to trust him.

'They could come,' the boy said, doubtfully. 'I suppose.'

'Merlin,' Teal said.

'Yes?'

'I'm not sure if we'll see each other again, after you've left this place. And I know it isn't going to be safe out there, whatever sort of ceasefire we end up with. But I want you to know two things.'

'Go on.'

'I'm glad you saved me, Merlin. If I never showed my gratitude until now ...'

'It wasn't needed. The war took too much from both of us, Teal. There was nothing else that had to be said. You'll do all right here, I know it. Maybe I'll drop back.'

'You know you won't,' Teal said. 'Just as you'll never go back to Plenitude.'

'And the other thing?'

'Take your ship, take your syrinx, and find your gun. For me. For your mother, your brother, for all the dead of Plenitude, for all the dead of the *Shrike*, for all who died here. You owe it to all of us, Merlin.'

He made to speak, but between one moment and the next he decided that words were superfluous. They met eyes for one last time, and an acknowledgement passed between them, a recognition of obligations met, duties faced, of good and bold hopes for better times.

Then he dropped out of the sensorium.

He was through into *Tyrant* in a matter of seconds. 'Get us out of here,' he said. 'Suspend all load ceilings. If I break a few bones, they'll just have to heal.'

'Complying,' *Tyrant* said.

Merlin's little dark ship was bruised and lame, but the acceleration still came hard and sudden, and he came very close to regretting that off-hand remark about his bones.

'When you have a chance,' he said, 'transfer Gallinule's sensorium through to the Iron Tactician. All of it – the whole of the Palace of Eternal Dusk.'

'While keeping a copy here, you mean?'

'No,' Merlin said. 'Delete it. Everything. If I ever need to walk those corridors again, or watch my mother looking sad, I'll just have to go back to Mundar.'

'That seems… extreme.'

'Tell that to Teal. She's made more of a sacrifice than I'll ever know.'

Tyrant punched its way through the thinning debris cloud. Merlin studied the navigation consoles, watching with a fascinated distraction as the ship computed various course options, testing each against the last, until it found what promised to be a safe passage to …

'No,' Merlin said. 'Not the Waynet. Not until we've gone back to Havergal and claimed that syrinx.'

'Did you not study the data, Merlin? I looked at it closely, after your inspection of the syrinx.'

'It's real.'

'Real, but damaged beyond safe use. More risky to use than the syrinx you already have. I'd have mentioned it sooner, but…'

'What do you mean, damaged?'

'Probably before Pardalote ever sold it on, Merlin. I doubt there was any intention to deceive. It's just that a broken syrinx is very hard to distinguish from a fully functioning one. Unless you've had quite a lot of experience in the matter.'

'And you kept that from me?'

'I was curious, Merlin. As were you. Another artificial intelligence. I thought we might at least see what this Iron Tactician was all about.'

Merlin nodded sagely. Occasionally he reached a point where he felt that little was capable of surprising him. But always the universe had something in store to jolt him out of that complacency. 'While we're on the subject, then. That little stunt you pulled back there, when I tried to shoot Struxer with the gamma-cannon...'

'You'd have come to regret that action, Merlin. I merely spared you endless years of racking remorse and guilt.'

'By contravening a direct order.'

'Which was foolish and unnecessary and born entirely out of spite. Besides, I was the damaged party, not you.'

Merlin brooded. 'I didn't know you had it in you.'

'Then we've both learned something new of each other, haven't we?'

He smiled – it was the only possible reaction. 'But let's not make too much of a habit of it, shall we?'

'On that,' *Tyrant* said, 'I think we find ourselves in excellent agreement.'

He felt the steering jets cut in, rougher than usual, and he thought about the damage that needed repairing, and the difficult days ahead. Never mind, though. Before he worried about those complications, he had a few small prayers to ask of his old, battered syrinx.

He hoped they would be answered.

About the Author

Alastair Reynolds was born in 1966 and has been writing science fiction full time since 2004, after leaving his career in space science. He has written fifteen solo novels, plus a collaboration with Stephen Baxter, and more than sixty short stories. He has been writing stories about the far future space traveller Merlin for nearly twenty years, of which "The Iron Tactician" is the latest.

Born in Wales, he has lived in Cornwall, Northumberland, Scotland and the Netherlands. He and his wife returned to Wales in 2008, where they live today surrounded by birds, trees and hills.

Selected Bibliography:

Revelation Space
1. Revelation Space (2000)
2. Chasm City (2001)
3. Redemption Ark (2002)
4. Diamond Dogs, Turquoise Days (2003)
4. Absolution Gap (2003)
5. The Prefect (2007)

Poseidon's Children
1. Blue Remembered Earth (2012)
2. On the Steel Breeze (2013)
3. Poseidon's Wake (2015)

Medusa Chronicles (with Stephen Baxter)
The Medusa Chronicles (2016)

Other Novels
Century Rain (2004)
Pushing Ice (2005)
House of Suns (2008)
Terminal World (2010)
Revenger (2016)

Collections:
Diamond Dogs, Turquoise Days (2002)
                              (Revelation Space Universe)
Zima Blue and Other Stories (2006)
Galactic North (2006) (Revelation Space Universe)
Thousandth Night and Minla's Flowers (2009)
Deep Navigation (2010)
Beyond the Aquila Rift: The Best of Alastair Reynolds (2016)

NewCon Press Novellas

Alastair Reynolds – The Iron Tactician

Simon Morden – At the Speed of Light

A tense drama set in the depths of space; the intelligence guiding a human-built ship discovers he may not be alone, forcing him to contend with decisions he was never designed to face.
Released January 2017

Anne Charnock – The Enclave

A new tale set in the same milieu as the author's debut novel "A Calculated Life", shortlisted for the 2013 Philip K. Dick Award. The Enclave: bastion of the free in a corporate, simulant-enhanced world…
Released February 2017

Neil Williamson – The Memoirist

In a future shaped by omnipresent surveillance, why are so many powerful people determined to wipe the last gig by a faded rock star from the annals of history? What are they afraid of?
Released March 2017

All cover art by Chris Moore.